CW00864645

KINDRED SPIRITS

ALLAN GILL

Copyright © 2016 Allan Gill
All rights reserved.

ISBN: 1530464730
ISBN 13: 9781530464739

PART 1

Flying Lessons

CHAPTER 1

The boy stood on the icy street corner hoarding his secret like a precious jewel. All around him the pavements were thronged with last minute Christmas shoppers, heads bowed against the wind, eyes studying their frozen feet as they waded through a sea of brown slush. The boy's feet were wet and cold too, but he ignored the discomfort. His eyes were raised to the darkening sky, tinted red with the threat of more snow. He didn't care about the weather, Christmas, how many angels could perch on a pinhead (though his secret had given him that knowledge), or anything else for that matter. His secret was far more important than any of the thousand trivial secrets swirling through the minds of the people scurrying past on their busy little errands. For he knew how to fly.

To accomplish this amazing feat he needed neither wings nor any other form of propulsion. In fact he could stand perfectly still, hands by his sides, and still be winging his way through blue, cloudless skies within seconds of take-off.

Take-off was achieved through the purchase of one small white pill from his supplier – another boy at the special school. The only problem was that he had to find the money to pay for his flying lessons and achieving that air-borne effect was becoming increasingly expensive.

Which was why Freddie Trench – for that was the boy's name - had spent most of this bleak December afternoon loitering with intent: An unnoticed scrap of humanity, frozen to the bone under the dingy Christmas lights on the corner of the litter-strewn high street.

"Ding dong merrily on high, Hosanna lives in Chelsea." He had been humming his own version of the seasonal ditty, in a vain attempt to maintain the festive spirit – and to stop his teeth chattering, when he spotted her.

The minute he clapped eyes on the young woman he knew she was the *one* and that his patience would be rewarded.

Victim: Twentysomething, middle-class blonde wearing an expensive-looking quilted jacket and a baseball cap with the pony-tail dangling out the hole. She had parked in a bus lane at the height of rush-hour traffic. No signal, no nothing. Just pulled up in her brand new shiny black Mitsubishi Shogun and jumped out, hair bobbing, to buy milk and a newspaper. Gridlock for a tabloid rag for heavens sake!

Oblivious to the driver she had carved up behind her, and all the other drivers behind him leaning on their horns as their blood pressure went through the roof.

Too busy unharnessing the brat from the front seat, then getting her purse out, (that was a pity) and making sure the hair bobbed just so as she jogged through the brown slush to the newsagent's, to worry about the mayhem she was causing.

Oblivious to the small, skinny kid with grungy jeans and the ring through his nose as he stood, like a phantom on the windswept corner pretending to read the yellowing ads in the shop window.

Equally oblivious to the fact that she had left the car keys in the ignition. Hadn't even taken time to turn the engine off.

Arrogance, he thought. No respect for anyone except herself, he thought. Deserves it, he knew. Well two fingers to you Mrs Cocky Blonde Baseball Cap.

Popping his last pill, he did a last check. She was in the shop, fourth in the queue with an old Asian bloke serving, and another three customers behind her all in a tight line, hemmed in by the tins of canned peas on one side and the nudey magazines on the other.

No chance. Oceans of time, even if she turned around and clocked what was happening, she had the baby to think about. Catch 22. Game, set and match, Mrs CBBC.

He made a final sweep up and down the busy street looking for a helmet. Not a sign. Bobbies on the beat were scarcer than hens' teeth at the best of times, and never around when you needed one. He stifled a giggle at the lame joke.

Maybe it was psychological, but the effect of the drug seemed to be kicking in already. He felt good. Not too spaced out. Just right. In control. Not flying yet, but reaching the summit of the world with the effortless ease of the addict. What was the phrase he had read in one of these glossy magazines - "express yourself" ? That was it, he was ready to express himself.

"Jingle bells, jingle bells, jingle all the way..." His tune changed as he sauntered ever so casually from the shop window to the kerb. Now he was sliding quietly behind and around the vehicle into the road.

He didn't look at the drivers' caught behind the Shogun. Rule number one. Never establish eye contact in the commission of a felony. It makes it easier for witnesses to remember your face and identify you in any subsequent police line-up.

But he could feel their anger and frustration coming in waves as thick as the pollution spewing out the exhaust pipes of their expensive motor cars. Their pent-up fury directed at anything that could move, while they were stuck in this god-awful traffic jam behind a rich, selfish woman too lazy to wait until she got home to her upper middle-class suburb to buy a newspaper. Don't worry guys, I'll have you on your way any minute now.

He took a big breath, wiped his damp palms on his jeans (that was funny, minutes before his hands had been freezing and now they were slick with sweat) – and opened the driver's door.

Moving quickly now. In. Pressing down the automatic door locks. Signalling. Turning the wheel. Leaving the kerb. From the corner of an eye, he sensed the commotion in the shop.

Baseball Cap thrusting her baby into the startled arms of the Asian shop-keeper. Milk down, paper thrown. Pushing through the queue. Shouting. Cursing.

Quick check in the rearview mirror. A large red face in a midnight blue Mercedes mouthing obscenities, while simultaneously attempting to push the horn through the steering column. He hauled the Shogun out into the oncoming traffic. A double-decker blared its horn, a black taxi joined the chorus. Jingle bells, jingle bells, jingle all the way.

Thump! Despite her petite build, Baseball Cap hit the door like a charging rhino. Screaming, kicking, smacking fists against the glass. The spit from her verbal assault misting the side window. Decision time. Abort, or control.

Express yourself. He pushed the lock release at precisely the same second she renewed her furious assault on the door handle. The passenger door flew open. Baseball Cap sat down with a look of stupefied surprise on her middle-class face and a dull, satisfying whump as her designer-jeaned bottom connected with the brown, slushy pavement. He leaned over, pulled the door shut, and screeched out of the bus lane into the chaotic traffic. Merry Christmas lady.

CHAPTER 2

Boom-boom, boom-boom, boom-boom, boom-boom. The beat of his pounding heart sounded huge in his ears, keeping pace with the car stereo's thumping rock anthem as the needle climbed northwards on the speedometer. Sixty-65-70-75….. Whooeee! These 4x4s were fast. Half an hour later and 15 miles from the crime scene, as the early evening gloom descended into darkness and the ecstasy-induced haze settled on his brain cells like a comfort blanket, Freddie relaxed, anticipating the night ahead.

A quick spin to Brighton – a club – pop a few more pills. Find a girl – maybe get lucky on the beach. Nah, too pebbly. More chance in the Shogun, but watch the upholstery. Don't want to give the dodgy car dealer any chance to drop his price.

Freddie would have been a bad kid in any town, but he had had far greater opportunity of expressing his criminality in a metropolis like London. Maybe he hadn't always been bad, like when he was a baby. After all how many bank robbers do you know under 18 inches tall, still in nappies, sticking up the cashier with a dummy, and using a buggy as the getaway car?

But by the time Freddie was five he had tried to set his granny on fire. She was snoring in her chair at the time and was only saved from incineration because her false teeth fell out wakening her up just as Freddie finally managed to light the matches. Tied a Catherine Wheel to the tail of a neighbour's dog. And poked out the eyes of his mum's pet goldfish with a lollipop stick, eh, while it was alive.

"Twisted nature" were the words the psychiatrists wrote in their reports to describe Freddie's behaviour. Perhaps it was in his genes. Not the ones you wear, dummy. Anyway, the spelling's completely different. No, what we're talking about here is the stuff inside you that makes you what you are. Freddie had heard stories about a great grandfather who had been hanged for a crime during the war. The subject was rarely mentioned, but when it was – in the occasional get-togethers with his cousins' in the East End - it was discussed by the grown-ups in the kind of shamed whispers reserved for a terrible family secret.

Freddie's mum also might have been a big reason for the horrible things he did. After all she was out most of the time – leaving him alone in the high rise flat. He didn't have a dad. And when she was home she was usually drunk, preferring fists to words when she got angry.

For the goldfish murder she punched him until his body was black and blue and locked him in his room all day without anything to eat or drink.

At the age of 12, Freddie finally had had enough of the beatings, stole £20 that his mum kept hidden under the mattress, peed on her bed, and threw her 16 inch television set out the window. They were 15 floors up. Although the TV was smashed to smithereens when it hit the concrete pavement 400 feet below, thankfully no one was injured.

That was the beginning of Freddie's downward spiral into real crime. Now – after shoplifting and stealing mobile phones from little kids – Freddie, at 15, had graduated to stealing cars.

No, wait a minute. Stealing was the wrong word. More accurately, Freddie had graduated to carjacking.

His undernourished chest thrust forward with pride in the Shogun's spacious driver's seat as he savoured the glamour of his latest crime. Carjacking. Felony of choice for the smarter young criminal. Tonight Freddie had become a trend- setter. Well, maybe not quite. Next time a Merc, or a Jag. Yeah, a Jag would definitely have him right up there among the elite of the Capital's most daring robbers.

But something was intruding on his daydream. A subliminal interference, like a tiny insect buzzing in a quiet room, was interrupting his good vibrations.

Light travels faster than sound. Freddie was aware of that elementary scientific fact, though he had never attended school long enough to take the class. His knowledge stemmed from the university of crime, where the senses had to be razor-sharp if you wanted to avoid detection and the eyes and ears were front-line weapons in the war of evasion. Right now, here came the imminent arrival of a practical lesson in light and sound that had far greater impact on Freddie than any laboratory experiment.

The whirling blue light in the Shogun's rearview mirror was travelling very fast and growing bigger with each passing second. Freddie's expert eye judged the police car was a couple of miles behind on the arrow straight stretch of dual carriageway.

They could be after anyone, ranging from a drink-driver spotted leaving a pub to the white van with the broken tail light that had piled past Freddie a few miles back. But they could also be after him. Thirty minutes was more than enough time for Mrs Baseball Cap to phone a cop shop from the Asian newsagent's, or from her own fancy mobile and get the forces of law an order mobilised (this time he didn't laugh at the pun) in the hunt for her prized possession.

Deciding it was better to be safe than sorry, he assumed he was the police target. Making an illegal U turn, which shred a centimetre of rubber from the Shogun's brand new tyres, he shot off up a side road parallel to the dual carriageway. As he executed the manoeuvre, he heard the first strident wail of the siren and did a quick double-take in his mirror.

The cop car had just run a red light half a mile away and was coming fast. Estimating that within the next sixty seconds he would know one way or the other, he forced himself down to 40 mph (never 30 – although that was the speed limit, nobody observed it and it would be a dead give-away, he reasoned.)

The police didn't need the dead give-away. Like a cruise missile homing in on target, the patrol car shot into the side road.

Requiring no second bidding, Freddie put his foot to the boards and the Shogun accelerated.

At the top of the road he threw the wheel right screeching into a long winding avenue of large self-contained houses partially hidden by hedgerows and lined on either side by a column of pine trees.

Fifty yards into the avenue he heard the same protesting squeal as the patrol car took the corner and, snatching another glimpse in the mirror, saw the copper in the passenger seat pulling the peak of his cap down.

Freddie pushed the Shogun harder – 70, 75, 80 – streaking past the tall oaks, silent sentinels to the desperate chase. The avenue widened slightly and became straighter. Under the sudden orange glare of a street light, Freddie saw it was a dead end.

Panic fluttered in his scrawny chest. He was going to get caught for sure this time and sent to a place much harder to break out of than the pansy special school. A place with barbed wire fencing, where he would have to start all over again and find a new pill supplier. All of that took time and he didn't have time to waste looking for a new source for his vital flying lessons. Once they dried up the winner that was Freddie Trench would dry up too.

He felt the sweat breaking out on his forehead and flicked another anxious glance up the long avenue.

The relief was instant, accompanied by a glorious feeling of exultation. He had been mistaken. It was a dead end as far as the road went all right. But in the darkness he could also make out a sign for a railway station pointing down a path and the silhouette of swings and a park – a large park fringed by the silent shadows of more trees.

Escape was less than 200 yards away. If he could make it to the park and ditch the car, a couple of fat bobbies would be no match for him in a foot race to the sanctuary of the path and the wood beyond. He smiled into the rearview mirror and gave them the finger as the Shogun leapt forward.

But the coppers' reaction was strange. Rather than showing frustrated rage, they were pointing wildly, screaming soundlessly through the windscreen now less than seventy yards behind him.

The truth dawned on Freddie a fraction of a second too late. As his head snapped from the mirror to the road ahead everything seemed to happen in slow motion inside the Shogun.

The second last thing he saw registered on the edge of his vision. The blurred image between the trees was of a whitewashed wall, dancing silver lights, and reflected in the waxen glow of a storm lamp, a giant winged shadow.

Astonished at the reality of his hallucination, the last thing failed 15-year-old carjacker Freddie Trench saw in this mortal world was the figure of what looked like a scarecrow flapping its arms in the middle of the road. He guessed he must finally be flying as the Shogun, losing speed but still travelling at 70 mph, smashed the scarecrow high into the air and careered off the road to bury itself in the centre of a mighty pine tree.

PART 2

Tumble Cottage

Chapter 3

Our first glimpse of Tumble Cottage was through winter skies. Driving sleet drilled black holes, like crows' eyes, in the glittering three day-old snow as it crystallised on the front lawn. A bone-chilling wind whistled through the pine trees surrounding the garden; whipping the drifts into half a dozen miniature powder storms amidst the branches, before lifting the snow once more and hurling it in waves of ghostly tumbleweed along the deserted avenue.

Corker was the first one out of our battered old people carrier – crunching up the path in her pink Pocahontas gumboots before Dad had even stopped the engine. Mum just managed to catch up with her as she was stretching to reach the large, iron horse-shoe door knocker. A good-luck symbol, I remember thinking at the time, as Mum grabbed the hand of my fiercely independent seven-year-old sister and I got my first proper look at the cottage that was to be our new home.

Well, it wasn't really a cottage by the time we arrived. It had originally been a cottage, but had been extended over the years by different owners until it was a proper family-size house just right for the five of us. The latest part of Tumble Cottage had been added only a couple of years before we moved in. It brought new bedrooms for my seven-year-old brother, Jamie, and me (in our old house he had been sharing with his twin sister Corker), a big kitchen – rather than the titchy one Mum used to cook in, and a huge lounge for Dad to hide in while he watches TV.

Everyone can see the changes shaped by bricks and mortar. For instance, nobody could possibly fail to notice a new school getting built, or another MacDonald's opening in your local high street. But there are changes happening to people and places going on around us all the time, which appear to be invisible to most grown-ups as they rush to work, rush to the pub, or, like my Dad, rush to sit down in front of the telly.

Corker, Jamie, and I, learned that important lesson when we moved into our new home a couple of weeks before Christmas during the snowiest winter in living memory.

The invisible changes I am talking about are not nice and cuddly like flying reindeer, or Santa getting stuck in the chimney. I wish they were. But this isn't the sort of story that makes you smile and wiggle your toes as you fall sleep. Not at all.

I don't believe that anyone else – except for us three children, particularly Corker (and maybe the old man, though we will never know for sure) – saw, *really saw,* the incredible things that happened during our first Christmas at Tumble Cottage.

Before we go ahead and knock on the front door, let me introduce my family and myself.

My name is Alex Madden. Despite the confusing first name, which sounds like a boy, I am a girl. I have long blonde hair, I'm 13 and a half (14 on February 18, next year), and I like clothes, singing, dancing, and hanging around with my mates – though not necessarily in that order. I have just started attending a new school called St Oliphants, which (you're right) sounds funny and is funny in a peculiar rather than amusing way with lots of geeky boys and old men teachers.

As I've already said, my brother, Jamie, and sister, Corker are seven-year-old twins. Mum says they were born within three minutes and twenty seconds of each other. She's always very precise on the time. Jamie came first – "screaming like a banshee", recalls Mum - and then Corker, blue and with hardly a whimper until the nurse held her up by the feet, "like a prize turkey", and slapped her on the bottom. Then she bawled until she turned from blue to beetroot red.

Anyway, the twins fight like cat and dog and are really entirely different – except that they obviously look alike, and sometimes have this weird habit of finishing each other's sentences. Mum says that's because they're from the same egg – part of the same yoke, as she describes it.

Jamie plays football and rugby at the weekends. He's a good tackler, but Dad, who jumps up and down on the touch line screaming, doesn't think he scores enough tries so he receives a pound for every one he gets (unfair!)) Jamie also attends Scouts and goes to Tumblewood First School.

Corker (our pet family name, she's really called Kristy) has brown hair and hazel eyes. One of them is slightly lazy, but Dad says that only makes her look even more beautiful (pass the sick bag please). Corker has just made her Brownie promise, and, like Jamie, also attends Tumblewood First School. In fact they're both in the same class.

We had a minor drama when the twins' started at Tumblewood because the head teacher, Miss Fullbright, put them in different classes. Miss Fullbright called it "a progressive experiment." Mum had another word for it, which I can't repeat here because it's swearing.

The progressive experiment ended abruptly one day when Corker threw a major tantrum in her class – they were doing art at the time - emptied the water from her paint pot all over her picture, and demanded to be taken to her brother because "he's hurt in the nurse's room."

When Corker's teacher finally relented, she found Jamie in the school secretary's office being sick in a bucket, while Mum was being phoned to come and collect him.

From then on the twins' shared the same class. They don't sit beside each other because, as I've said, they argue most of the time. But they seem to be more comfortable in the same room. Which is why – despite the fact that they can now have a bedroom each at Tumble Cottage – they still prefer to sleep together in the same room.

It's maybe that egg and yoke idea Mum talks about. She says they get "peace of mind" from simply knowing the other one's okay. Even Miss Fullbright seems to have learned that lesson because when Dad handed in their application form for junior school, she said they would definitely be in the same class when they go there next September.

Dad writes a bit, teaches a bit, and sits around a lot drinking beer and watching sports programmes on TV, which is boring for us because we never get to see our favourite programmes like Hollyoaks, EastEnders, Emmerdale, or Coronation Street. At the moment he is even grumpier than usual as he isn't allowed to drink beer because Mum has put him on a diet.

Mum works very hard for a big company and has to travel abroad for a few days nearly every week. In fact it was her job that made us move from our old house in Yorkshire to Tumble Cottage, which is in Surrey. Anyway, I was saying that Mum has to go away a lot. So by the time she gets back on a Friday, she's exhausted, and we order home delivery pizza and get to pig out in front of TV at least an hour later than our usual bedtime. So we are very much your average, normal family.

But this story doesn't really involve Mum and Dad. For some reason (as we also mentioned before, maybe its because they're adults and as Corker says, not as "sentitive" as children) they never saw anything. And Jamie, Corker and I made a pact never to tell them because we knew if they ever found out we would all be out of Tumble Cottage faster than it takes to say abracadabra and, despite all that has happened, we still like the place.

Mum does too. But then she liked the look of the house the instant she saw the photographs in the estate agent's window, and I guess she fell in love with it on that first visit from the moment she raised the iron horse-shoe and knocked on the door.

CHAPTER 4

The vibrations caused by the knocker set a string of silver fairy lights dancing above the solid oak door, and a thick wedge of snow fell silently from a window ledge scoring a direct hit on Dad's head as he trod up the path.

We were all laughing our socks off – and Dad was still cursing and hopping up and down trying to get the snow off the back of his neck – when the door opened.

A small woman, with tiny, round spectacles and dark, greasy hair styled in the fashion of a pudding bowl, stood before us.

The estate agent had already warned Mum and Dad that the owners of Tumble Cottage – a middle-aged Polish couple called Mr and Mrs Pelejic could be what he termed "pretty nippy" – particularly the woman. From the estate agent's description, this could only be the formidable Mrs P. Dad later declared her manners not so much nippy as "positively frosty".

Certainly, the sight of my father shaking himself like a demented dog, while the rest of our family howled at his antics like a pack of hyenas, did nothing to melt her glacial reception.

Perhaps it was the canine image that put her off. For Mrs P turned out to be very keen on cats. The stench that filled our nostrils as we crossed the doorstep betrayed that fact even before she opened her mouth.

Marshalling us on our inspection of Tumble Cottage, Mrs P began in the tones of a professional tour guide. Later in the people carrier, Dad offered the opinion that she had had plenty practice showing people around as the house had been on the market so long because of the "extortionate price" the Pelejics' wanted for it.

Mrs P revealed that the cottage was originally built in the 1930s – only a few years before the Second World War. "An army colonel once lived here," she informed us, thrusting her chin proudly in the air as we looked around one of the two and a half tiny bedrooms that comprised the original sleeping quarters for Tumble Cottage.

"He was second in command to Monty at El Alamein. Our old gardener used to garden for the colonel as well. He told us he had maps of the battles hanging all over the walls. Do *you* know about the famous Field Marshal Montgomery? Have you heard of the Battle of El Alamein?" she asked looking at Jamie.

Behind the round spectacles her small, bird-like eyes, studied my brother as though he was a scientific specimen. "Is it a war film?" he asked nervously. "Pah." Mrs P gave a disgusted sniff as if she had just become aware of the cat stink. "War film. That's all children know about – films and video games. Nothing about history, nature, or the environment. That's one of the reasons why Mr Pelejic and I never wanted them."

Instead of children Mrs Pelejic had cats. "Twelve!" she exclaimed in a loud, boastful voice as we entered the smallest bedroom and the principle source of the horrible smell. "I have 12. As you can see, I keep them in here. The heating boiler's in the cupboard over there. It's the warmest room in the house, so they stay nice and snugly, buggly warm through the night. Don't you my babies."

Mrs P's professional tour guide voice had collapsed into gurgling baby noises. Recognising the voice of their mistress, half a dozen of the cats rose from their litter to circle Mrs P, purring and stretching luxuriously as they rubbed their backs against her legs.

Her mood darkened like the flick of a light switch the minute we left the cat bedroom. "I had 13, but Tinkles died tragically," she confided as we descended the stairs. "Run over by some boy racer outside our own front door. Most of the time the road's as quiet as the grave, but you have to watch these boy racers," she said, hissing the last words like a curse. "Just to let you know, he's buried in the back garden. I'll show you where, so the children don't dig him up. I do hope you like animals."

For an instant we had a chilling vision of the boy racer occupying a plot under the petunias rather than the tragic Tinkles, until Mrs P confirmed that the cat killer had escaped with "a piffling" four hours community service for his crime.

Fortunately Mr Pelejic was not buried in the garden either, though he looked pale and drawn with a head sprouting only the occasional anaemic tuft of white hair and later, in the car, Dad pronounced him "not long for this world" – adding the ominous sounding word "leukaemia".

Perhaps somehow aware of Dad's prophecy, Mr P made himself scarce during our visit leaving his formidable wife to show us round.

Despite the "extortionate price", mum saw what she called its "potential" – and, being a gardening addict, she saw even more potential in the garden. So we bought Tumble Cottage and moved in just two weeks before Christmas.

Mum and Dad had taken time off work to get unpacked and generally settle us all into our new surroundings. But before we could begin shifting furniture we had to deal with the legacy of the Pelejics.

"Mean. Meaner than Scrooge. I bet they're related to the old codger on the Polish side of the family!" Dad was shouting at the top of his voice and he sounded like he was blowing a gasket. We were all accustomed to his ravings, but he sounded particularly mad about something as the three of us headed towards the source of the outburst.

We found him in the lounge half way up a ladder examining a short strand of cable hanging out of the wall, while Mum listened patiently to his raging.

"Live. These wires are live. They're so tight they took the blasted lights and left live wires. I've never seen anything like it in my life. They knew we had children too. The kids could be electrocuted, but do they care? We'll be in the dark until we can get an electrician. They shouldn't be allowed to get away with it. We should phone their solicitor. Stop the cheque until they replace the lights. What do you think?"

Mum stood, hands on hips, nodding in agreement. She knew all about Dad's use of the word "we". When he said "we" he actually meant Mum should leap into action and phone the solicitor.

The Pelejics' miserly streak had been evident from the moment we arrived that morning just ahead of the large blue removal truck with the legend "Quickflit – fast and efficient movers" - emblazoned in flaming red and gold letters on the side. The iron horse-shoe door knocker had been replaced with something cheap and nasty that looked and sounded like tin, prompting Dad's first fit of the day.

Leaving Dad to stamp around in circles, Mum got on with directing operations. Standing in the hall like a traffic cop, she stopped, signalled, and waved the sweating men on from Quickflit as they lugged wardrobes, beds, tables, chairs and, of course, boxes and boxes of toys to various points around the house.

Needless to say, Mum got the job done in record time. While Dad – after making several cups of tea for himself and the removal men – was still trying to decide where to start on the massive task of fumigating the house. The one thing the Pelejics' had left behind was the malodorous stench of her cats.

There was an ulterior motive to Mum's industry, which we discovered as the Quickflit truck departed with a belch of diesel fumes and a scrunch of tyres down our driveway. "Sshh," she said putting her hands to her lips. "Your Dad will be hours in there fussing and fuming. Let's leave him to it. Get your gumboots on and we'll explore the garden."

So with the sound of Dad's curses ringing in our ears as he raged about "filthy beasts" while he scrubbed the cat bedroom floor on all fours, we tip-toed our way outside.

This time our sour tour guide Mrs P was absent and we were truly free to enjoy the pleasures of the place without the restriction of having to mind our Ps and Qs under her beady eye. It was a wonderful feeling.

First, Mum carried out a quick inventory of what was in the front garden. It was difficult for her to identify too many of the plants or bushes that would flower the following summer because of the snow. But she managed to spot a large camellia bush by the study wall. A slender eucalyptus tree weaved delicate shadows across the storm lamp at the front door, while a hanging basket looked forlorn above the kitchen window without the riot of colour it would become in summer.

The front lawn was about 40 feet long, rolling gently down to the pavement and fenceless at the bottom. It reminded me of the front lawns we had seen on holiday in America, so I liked it immediately. Two large pine trees stood on either side of the driveway and a third was positioned at the bottom of the garden opposite the long line of pines bordering the street. Clumps of rhododendron bushes and azaleas flanked either side of the garden alongside waist high hedges.

The front looked pretty, but it wasn't nearly so big or interesting as the back garden. It was far larger than the pocket-handkerchief sized garden we were used to in Yorkshire and Jamie had christened it "a park" when he had first seen it on tour with Mrs P. It was more than 200 feet long and arranged in three distinct sections.

The first part directly outside the house was a lawn fringed by high copper beech hedges and more rhododendron bushes. About 50 feet down the lawn a semi-circle of fir trees almost completely obscured the rest of the garden from the house. Here a single line of crazy paving stones cut a pathway through the middle of a wildly overgrown area of flowers and bushes.

Beyond this "jungle", the second section was again a discrete garden in its own right consisting of a mixture of flowerbeds and high bushes with a giant broken oak covered in ivy marking the border. The third section was also about fifty feet in length featuring longer, wilder grass and bounded by a series of silver beech trees, which provided privacy from the large secondary school just over the fence. The bottom of our long garden was by far the most interesting area because of two distinct features.

The first, Mum discovered as she led our reconnaissance party on that winter afternoon.

"Look at the footprints. What kind of animal do you think made them?" she asked pointing at a line of marks in the snow that led directly towards a thick clump of bushes in the left corner of the garden. "Not more stinky, blinking cats Mum," said Jamie with a note of resigned exasperation that only a world-weary seven-year-old can muster.

"No. Look closer. What do you see Alex?" I looked and saw nothing more than Jamie had managed to come up with.

"The prints are too big for a cat," said Mum. "It looks to me like we've had a visit from Mr Reynard. "A fox," explained Mum, registering our blank looks.

"A fox. Wow. Cool," breathed Corker. Mum followed the tracks to the bushes and, hunkering down, pushed the foliage carefully aside. "Aha, just as I thought. Come and have a look at this," she said waving us over enthusiastically. "Now let's be careful and not disturb anything, or we might frighten them off," she said as we joined her. Parting the branches again, she pointed at a hole tunnelled into a mound of earth, which was about eight feet long stretching back to the school fence. "I think we've found the foxes house," whispered Mum. "Wicked," Jamie whispered back. "Do you think they're in?" "I don't know," laughed Mum, "but if we want them to stay our neighbours we better not touch anything." We stared at the hole for several minutes willing the emergence of Mr Reynard, but to no avail. "Even if they are in there they won't come out when we are around. They're scared of humans," said Mum.

Next to the foxes house was a shed, where Mum intended storing all of her gardening tools and her pride and joy – the new fire-engine red garden tractor she had bought specially to sit in and mow the "park" when spring arrived.

The other interesting feature lay at the bottom of the garden in the opposite corner from the shed. Like the foxes' lair, it was also a house of sorts. Only it was the strangest house I had ever seen. For a start it looked far too small for anybody to actually live in – even Corker had to bend down in order to try and get through the entrance. The roof was made of rusty iron with big bolts and sloped down like an igloo. The walls were brick without any windows, and the front door looked as if it might fall down at any minute.

"Is it a Wendy House from the olden days?" asked Corker. "Don't be stupid, Corks, it's a garden shed," I scoffed in my most know-all big sister voice.

"Alex! Don't speak to your little sister as if she's an idiot," said Mum. "For your information Madam, it's an air-raid shelter."

"Was that to do with bombs and stuff?" asked Jamie, his attention now fully engaged. "That's right Jamie. During the Second World War we fought the Germans and they sent planes to bomb London. So people living in this part of the country had to leave their houses and stay in shelters like this in order to be safe while the bombs were being dropped."

"How much bombs did the Germans drop?" asked Jamie.

"Many. How many bombs did the Germans drop," corrected Mum. "I'm sorry I don't know the answer to that one, but it would be thousands."

"Let's look inside, there could be an unexploded bomb," enthused Jamie.

"Could there Mum?" I asked, automatically retreating a couple of steps.

"No, of course not, Jamie's been watching too many war films," said Mum.

"Then what are we waiting for," said Jamie marching towards the door.

"No not now," said Mum. "It's too dark to see properly. Anyway it's starting to snow. We'd better get back to the house. "

As if in greeting, Dad's outraged tones came floating down the garden through the falling flakes. "You won't believe this. They've even taken the toilet roll holder off the bathroom wall."

Chapter 5

It didn't stop snowing for the rest of the evening and we stared out on the storm from the warmth of our new home with a mixture of fascination and excitement.

Mum was tucking us up in bed when Corker suddenly sat bolt upright, tears welling in her eyes. "Mum. What about the foxes? They'll starve to death in this weather. We'll have to feed them."

So it was that we found ourselves trooping in single file down the garden behind the glow of Mum's torch to deliver a midnight feast of leftover pizza to the fox family.

Early next morning Mum's excited voice summoned us to the big lounge. Hushing us with a warning finger to her lips, she pointed down the garden. At first we could see nothing, but as our eyes adapted to the dazzling whiteness of the landscape, gradually the reason for Mum's excitement took shape. In the snowbound silence beyond the drooping fir trees we suddenly detected a movement – a limp brown tail sticking out from behind a bush. Then the owner of the tail emerged. His sharp face turned automatically towards the house and the eyes – alert for the merest sign of danger – seemed to look straight at us.

"Rat's Tail," whispered Corker clutching Mum's hand. "It's Rat's Tail from the Reynard family."

That's how the first of our fox family neighbours got his name. Standing still as statues, our breath steaming up the frozen lounge windows, we glimpsed the other two family members. With an explosion of powder and crystals the second fox tumbled from a bush alongside Rat's Tail. We heard the muted sound of a sneeze as he shook the snow from his fur to reveal a rich red coat. For no apparent reason he suddenly leapt in the air and then attempted to chase his own tail – a considerably bushier affair than the one Rat's owned. Mum christened this chap Youngblood.

The final member of the family could hardly have been more different from the young whippersnapper we watched gambolling in the snow like a puppy.

When Old Mangy appeared (for that was the name we later gave the third fox) there was no mistaking that he was the head of the family. He emerged much more slowly from his hiding place than his relatives. Part of the reason was because he was clearly old. He had a limp in one of his back legs and his coat was threadbare in patches and streaked with grey in others. But despite his age and injury, there was an unmistakable dignity in Old Mangy's bearing. Not once did he look in our direction. Instead his nose rose imperiously sniffing the chill air for what could only have been a minute, but seemed like an age as we held our breaths. Then satisfied that he had scented humans, but equally certain that we were far enough away to allow a dignified retreat, he nodded his head once before hobbling slowly back towards the bottom of the garden.

Rat's Tail immediately took the hint and sloped off after Mangy. But Youngblood capered in a snowdrift for several more minutes before finally realising he was alone and – with a final sneeze and shake of his brushy tail, he darted back through the trees to the safety of his burrow. Of course the Reynard family had demolished all of our offerings. Dad, semi-joking but at the same time making a serious point, told us that foxes were "scavengers" and would eat just about anything. "We shouldn't encourage them by leaving food out. It only means they will be doing their disgusting doings all over the garden and I'm not cleaning it up," he moaned. Mum led our booing as he made a grumpy retreat and, despite Dad's objections, we all resolved to keep up the daily food offerings.

Apart from delivering our scraps to the Reynard family, the weather was so bad that we hardly ventured over the doorstep during the next few days.

Most of our time was taken up exploring every inch of our new home. Jamie was particularly keen to track down the colonel's famous battle maps and plagued Dad until he was forced to lead an expedition up the folding metal ladders into the loft.

The light didn't work and there was a sudden very smart retreat down the ladders when Dad stumbled across a large white sphere the size of a football. He identified the object, in an uncharacteristically small voice, as a wasp's nest.

After donning a ski suit zipped snugly at the chin and ankles, a woolly hat over his ears, gloves, goggles, and tying a tea towel round his face, Dad armed himself with a ski pole and clutching a bin bag, he ventured into the loft once more. "Your Dad looks like he's about to walk on the moon," giggled Mum as we crowded together on the landing below. The loft went eerily quiet for what seemed like a very long time. I counted the dust motes, caught in the sunlight, as they floated down from the black gaping mouth that was the hatch. I wondered if Dad had found something monstrous in the loft, like a gigantic mutant wasp, and been eaten alive.

"Landing to loft, this is mission control. Are you receiving us," Mum said in a voice that was meant to be funny, but sounded slightly nervous. There was a sudden scraping followed by what sounded like Dad cursing, though we couldn't be sure because of the tea towel. "Ugger, I've umped my ead on a eam." Then, after a much shorter period of radio silence, the muffled commentary resumed and, as our hearing became more attuned to the distortion caused to Dad's voice by Mum's tea towel, we managed to decipher "a ear" as "all clear" and "ook it" as "look out."

Dad's legs shot through the hatch above us and we rapidly cleared a path as he came charging down the steps holding the black bin bag well away from himself as if it contained a bomb about to explode. "It's okay, I'm pretty certain they're all dead. Too cold up there," he said as he pulled the tea towel down and moved smartly downstairs with the outstretched bag. "But better to be on the safe side, I'll just bury it at the bottom of the dustbin."

Apart from the unexpected excitement of the wasp's nest, the loft turned out to be a big let down. The discovery of two very dusty, rusty brown trunks caused a flurry of activity for a couple of minutes with Jamie talking Dad's ear off about his new best friend Monty and El Alamein. But when Dad finally managed to open them - with the help of a torch and a crowbar - all they contained was more dust.

As the days went by we settled into our home and into the routine of new schools. The weather remained cold and changeable. Some days were bright with winter sunshine, others were overcast with the threat of more snow in the air.

Every Christmas mum hangs up an Advent calendar on the 1st of December. She always buys one with chocolates hidden in little boxes behind each date and the three of us take it in turn to open the boxes every day. But this particular Christmas she had been so busy with the move that she only remembered to buy a calendar on the 15th of December with ten days to go to the big event. It didn't really spoil it for us. In fact – even the incredible things that happened didn't spoil that Christmas. Somehow they made it more special – and getting to open five days worth of chocolates each to bring us up to date with the calendar, certainly got the Christmas period off to a great start.

Maybe it was too good because I wakened in the middle of the night curled into a ball, teeth chattering.

CHAPTER 6

At first I blamed it on too many chocolates, or thought I was about to come down with some horrible bug. Then I discovered that I had kicked my duvet off the bed.

The luminous red numbers on my digital radio glowed 11.30 and I groaned as I pulled the duvet over my head and turned over again. But it was no use, try as I might I couldn't get back to sleep and the drone of a plane didn't help either. I listened as the engines gradually grew louder overhead and, maddeningly, found my brain instructing my ears to strain for the last dying echoes as it passed.

The Gatwick flight path was hardly an ideal remedy for insomnia, I thought, and wondered whether Mum and Dad had paid enough attention to the location of the airport before buying Tumble Cottage.

The absence of curtains on my window added to the problem. Mum hadn't gotten round to putting them up and a full moon provided an irritatingly constant night light as it shone unwavering in a starless black sky.

Wrestling with the bedclothes until the luminous numbers showed 12.00, I finally gave up and decided I needed to go to the toilet. It was as I tiptoed along the landing, carefully avoiding the creaky floorboard outside Mum and Dad's bedroom, that I sensed something move. The landing felt colder and I was suddenly wide- awake.

Somehow I knew the movement wasn't inside the house and that made me braver. Steeling myself, I peered out the hall window into the front garden.

Deserted. Nothing there but the familiar snow-shrouded shapes in their usual places. The big bush by the study window Mum had called a camellia, the smaller, as yet unidentified bush in the middle, and the lawn stretching white and empty down to the pine trees fringing the edge of the garden. I gave a mighty sigh of relief not even realising that I had been holding my breath.

As I moved to the toilet I suddenly saw the figure through the pines illuminated by the street lamp. It was in profile, muffled from head to foot in a long coat with a scarf masking the face, and a hat pulled down over its head. It was impossible to tell whether it was male or female, but I was certain it was very old as it moved painfully slowly in small, shuffling steps. However, apart from the lateness of the hour, perhaps the most peculiar thing was that the figure was wandering up the middle of the road.

I froze, heart thumping, I squeezed my eyes tight shut, praying the creature would not look up and see me. When I opened them again, which could only have been a second later, the figure was gone.

My imagination caught fire with a stream of awful possibilities. What if it was a burglar, a car thief, or worse – a murderer? Should I wake up my parents? Alert the neighbours? Phone the police?

For a nanosecond I considered going downstairs, unchaining the front door and venturing outside to see if I could catch another glimpse of the figure. But the mere thought of walking across the empty lawn and down to the trees – trees behind which any kind of monster could be lurking – made me whimper.

Another awful possibility struck me. What if the thing circled behind me and went through the open door into the house and upstairs to my bedroom while I was investigating outside?

No thanks. I am not the sort of person who would ever go into a cellar to check whether an axe murderer is there. Even at the age of 13, I have seen enough horror movies to know that anyone who is stupid enough to do that always comes to a sticky end.

Instead, I stared at the spot under the street light for what seemed an age, but the figure did not re-appear. I began to wonder if I had actually seen anything at all. It could have been a trick of the lighting – the shadow of a branch waving in the wind. Trees can bend into weird and wonderful shapes at night. I looked out the window again, examining the pines.

But there was no movement. The night was as still as the grave. I shuddered at the thought of graves and felt goosebumps rising on my bare arms. I went quickly to the toilet and ran back through the cold hall - without so much as a sideways glance out the window – and dived shivering under the duvet.

CHAPTER 7

Luckily for me next day was an inset day at St Oliphants', so I was allowed to lie-in, while Jamie and Corker were packed off to school. I heard them squabbling downstairs – "Why's *she* allowed to stay off, it's unfair, she'll eat sweets and watch TV"- as Mum struggled to keep the peace and make the lunch boxes at the same time. I was exhausted after my disturbed night, but the delicious sound of the twins' complaining about my day off was like music to my ears and I drifted off into a contented, dreamless sleep.

"Wake up lazy bones. Look at the time. You're missing a lovely day." Mum was at the foot of the bed with her gardening gloves on shaking my legs. "Come on. It's 10.30. Get dressed and come and help me in the garden."

Gardening is not exactly my idea of having fun. The twins' earlier observations were entirely accurate. My favourite pastimes involve eating sweeties, and watching TV – strictly in that order of priority. But, as I showered and had a quick bowl of Frosties, I knew there would be no getting off the hook. Mum's command, drifting up from the bottom of the garden, only confirmed the fact that it might be an inset day for the teachers', but it was also going to be a green fingers day for Alex Madden.

"Come on Alex. Get your lazy bottom down here. It's a wonderful morning." Pulling on my navy blue Italia tracksuit top and new Nike trainers, I trudged reluctantly outside to find Mum in her element piling dead branches from an area of rough paving stones into a wheelbarrow. From there she was ferrying them to the beginnings of a bonfire – as yet unlit – in the far corner of the garden.

Hands jammed into my grey Nike tracksuit bottoms, I kicked the snow, and Mum raised her head from her work. Her smile turned into a frown and I knew what was coming.

"Oh come on Alex. This isn't a fashion show. Get changed into some old clothes and come and help me. And you can get that sullen look off your face madam, or you'll be grounded this weekend."

Normally, I would have put up much stouter resistance. Scowled a lot more, and infuriated her by asking loads of stupid questions about what kind of clothes she meant – although I knew perfectly well all along. I find those kind of tactics usually do the trick and get me out of chores as Mum simply gets tired of asking and sends me to my room instead, which is fine because I can play my music. But this weekend I wanted to see a couple of my friends, so I decided that it was in my best interests to be good.

Replacing my scowl and Italia top with an old sweater, jeans and gumboots, I presented myself again in a suitably agreeable mood.

And, I would never admit it to Mum, but as I helped fill the wheelbarrow with branches, I actually started to enjoy myself.

A Robin Redbreast joined us as we worked. He fluttered from the bare branches of an apple blossom tree to perch cheekily on the handle of the wheelbarrow. His head cocked to one side, eyes bright with enquiry, as if at any second he was about to ask: *What on earth are you humans doing?*

A jet passed high overhead. Its vapour trail carved a long white slash in the canvas of a brilliant blue winter sky, as it climbed from Gatwick to some exciting destination. Mum was right, it was a beautiful morning.

The raucous jangle of the school bell jolted me out of my reverie and we continued to work to the accompaniment of the screams and gibbering laughter of the playground jungle just over the fence.

It took us eleven trips with the wheelbarrow to gather all the branches from the paving stones. It took almost as many matches to light the bonfire and, even then, the flames flickered weakly and the smoke rose in lazy cigar-shaped wisps on the bright, chill air.

By that time playtime was over and a welcome silence reigned again. After Mum finished sweeping the remaining twigs from the paving stones, we had a break for a cup of tea - somehow tea always tastes a thousand times better outside - and a chocolate biscuit, which tastes great anywhere.

Then she announced we were moving on to tidy up the shelter because she wanted somewhere dry to store logs for the fire. (Building great roasting fires in the lounge is another one of her favourite pastimes, she's weird is my Mum.) The news came as no surprise as Mum never does anything by half measures, especially gardening. I expected myself to groan, instead I relished the idea.

Although I had seen the shelter from the outside, the weather had been too cold and wet for anything other than the most cursory inspection. This would be the first proper exploration and, like any slightly horrible big sister, I enjoyed the thought of beating Jamie and Corker to it, even more the prospect of winding them up about what they had missed while they were at school.

Of course, I kept my mischievous plans from Mum as she would have banned me immediately had she known. We started by moving the door out of the way. It had long since come off its rusty hinges and was lying inside the entrance. Originally it looked as if it had been painted green, but most of the paint had weathered away and the bare wood looked black and rotten. The rotten part was confirmed the instant we lifted the door. It felt as light as a feather and a large chunk came away in Mum's gardening gloves as she transferred it to the bonfire.

Beyond the door lay a mound of course blankets with black and red stitching around the outside. I had seen the same kind of blankets when we visited Grandma's house in Edinburgh. Because she didn't have enough duvets for everybody, she brought the blankets out when we slept over. They were itchy and went under something called a candlewick bedspread. Heaven knows why because there were no candles on the covers. Anyway, there were no candlewick bedspreads in the shelter. The itchy blankets were enough for Mum. She screamed and I just about leapt out of my skin as the biggest spider I had ever seen emerged from one pile and went skittering across the floor into the shelter's darkest recesses. She kicked the pile several times and shoved it across the floor with her foot to smoke out any other creepy crawly surprises before hastily despatching the pile to the bonfire.

With the blankets removed we could now see four tea chests. Mum made a brief attempt to move one, but gave up immediately, muttering about slipped discs. She declared they were far too heavy for even both of us to shift and so we began to empty the contents.

The first one was full of newspapers. The top copies crumbled to dust in our hands as we lifted them. But as we delved deeper the newspapers – although faded – were intact. One yellowing headline, dated 1941, read "A Night That Nearly Took The Heart Out Of London" and the black and white picture beneath showed a pall of smoke surrounding a church called St Paul's Cathedral.

Further down the pile another newspaper from 1942 had the headline "Monty Scores Triumph At El Alamein" with a picture of a very serious-looking soldier in a tank wearing a beret and a moustache and holding a pair of binoculars. The caption below read "General Montgomery poses before the battle commences."

"Mum is that the man Mrs P was talking about. That Monty and El Alamein?" I asked excitedly. Mum nodded as she picked another batch of newspapers from the tea chest. "Yes. Only you notice he was called General then. He must have been promoted to the higher rank of Field Marshall after he won the battle."

"I wonder if we'll find any maps for Jamie," I said delving deeper into the pile.

But the first two tea chests only contained old newspapers. I thought Mum would burn the lot on the bonfire as we found quite a few more creepy crawlies hiding in the papers and a lot more scurrying around the bottom of the boxes. However, she carefully separated the papers in good condition from the ones that crumbled to dust. "We'll put these in the loft Alex," she said solemnly. "They tell a very important story in this country's history. The people who lived here over sixty years ago when all these terrible things were happening obviously felt it was important to keep these newspapers. Out of respect for them I think we should do the same. Don't you?"

I wasn't exactly sure what Mum was talking about. But when our history teacher, an ancient old duffer called Mr Hogarth, spoke about the war tears came into his eyes. And he was the strictest teacher at St Oliphants. So I guessed it must be important and nodded agreement with Mum.

We never found any of the colonel's battle maps that chilly December day. But as the bonfire sparked and smouldered on, and the sun gradually went down in the winter sky, the air raid shelter gave up other long forgotten treasure.

The third tea chest revealed a collection of metal plates, rusty knives and forks, and what seemed like an unending selection of unopened tins containing such exotic items as spam, corned beef and pilchards. There was a box of crumbling Oxo cubes, a bottle of coffee with a colour picture of a Highland soldier sitting in a kilt being served by an Indian servant, another bottle containing a suspicious brown mud-like liquid called Garton's HP Sauce, and an incredible variety of powdered foods. Powdered milk, egg powder, custard powder and even potato powder. I never realised so many things could be made from powder and wondered what they would taste like. "Wait until Corker sees these, they'll be great for playing shops," I enthused, studying the tins' labels featuring the beaming, rosy-cheeked faces of boys and girls from another age.

"I'm sorry sweetheart," said Mum. "The tins will be too dangerous for Corker and you to play with. Anything inside them will have gone bad years ago and I can't take the chance of them opening accidentally – or Corker opening them on purpose. You know what she's like Alex." My protests were faint-hearted because – although I was disappointed that we wouldn't be able to play shops with this exotic food store from a bygone age – I knew that Mum had gotten it exactly right where Corker was concerned. My little sister was forever experimenting with Mum's make-up – grinning from ear to ear as she traipsed downstairs with huge clown lips smeared on in lipstick. Only a few weeks earlier, Mum and Dad had gone ballistic and sent her to bed early when they discovered her trying to trim her eyebrows with a pair of scissors.

And Mum did relent on the plates and knives and forks saying that she might allow us to play houses with them – after they were boiled.

The most exciting discoveries – certainly from Jamie's point of view – came in the third chest. The moth-eaten haversack was jammed in a corner. Inside it we found a soldier's helmet coloured a drab olive green and a matching water bottle. The helmet would be fine for playing soldiers. But, like the tins, the water bottle would have to disappear Mum said because Jamie was just about as daft as Corker and I could imagine his own special supply of Diet Coke going straight into the unwashed bottle.

The final chest looked like being a spectacular let-down. We spent the first few minutes removing two layers of bricks and Mum cursed and hopped around like a dervish doing a war dance when she dropped one on her foot.

At first glance the tarpaulin under the bricks didn't appear much more exciting. But when we unwound the plastic sheeting a black box fell onto the grass. At least the object looked like a box until Mum turned it over revealing a series of knobs on the front, a dial, and a semi circle of straw-coloured mesh.

"Why it's an old wireless," she said. "They didn't have any TV seventy years ago you know Alex. Instead families in those days would huddle around the wireless for their entertainment – and to listen to the news. Particularly news about how the war was going."

"The war with the Germans you mean," I said twiddling the knobs and hearing nothing but the mechanical click as they turned on and off. We had been studying the Second World War with Mr Hogarth throughout that term and were up to the Blitz. "But what's the wireless doing down here mum?"

"The people who lived here during the war must have listened to the wireless when they took cover in the shelter during the air raids."

"When London got bombed?"

"That's right, but although London was the main target for the German bombers other places got hit too all over this part of England."

Next out came an old lamp. Over the years one side had been squashed flat under the weight of the bricks and the frame was covered in a film of rust. "Where's the bulb?" I asked as Mum scraped it with her shears to reveal the dull sheen of metal. "There is no bulb. They had no electricity here at the bottom of the garden. It's an oil lamp. You poured oil in and lit it with matches."

An old pack of playing cards lay scattered on the bottom of the chest. Instead of having hearts and diamonds, or Kings and Queens they had pictures of Spitfires, Hurricanes, Stukas and Messerschmitts. "War planes," said Mum. "It must have been a card game like Happy Families, only instead of Mr Bun the Baker they played snap with bombers and fighter planes."

"Yuck!" My exclamation of disgust was aimed at the last item Mum held up gingerly between her thumb and forefinger barely touching the handle. "It's a potty", she said. "You must remember, they often had to stay here for hours at a time. This became their second home. They couldn't run back to the bathroom during an air raid, so they had to be prepared for every little eventuality."

Thankfully the shuddering embarrassment of having to do the toilet in front of other people, even if they were your family, passed almost immediately as my attention was caught by something else sticking out of the folds of the tarpaulin.

I picked up the old photograph very carefully. It was dog-eared and its sepia-tinted colour was fading. But I could still make out the faces of a family staring solemnly out of the photograph, dressed in their Sunday best for the camera. The mother and father were at the back of the picture.

The man was tall and stood ramrod straight with a black moustache so thick and bristling it looked as though it might fly out of the picture and attack us. He was wearing an army officer's uniform with a row of ribbons and medals across his chest. A peaked cap emphasised his sharp features and knee-high boots completed the image of importance. Although he dwarfed the woman at his side, she appeared equally striking with a darkness to her hair and eyes that the faded brown and white of the old photograph could not dim. She held a baby in her arms. It could only have been weeks or months old, judging from the tiny nature of the bundle, which was almost completely obscured by blankets. A lanky boy of about ten, his hair in a cow-lick, wearing a V-neck pullover and matching shorts with incredibly skinny legs poking out the ends, stood at the front. He seemed uncertain whether to laugh or scowl.

"That photo was taken right here. Look, the lilac tree is behind them – though the fence, and the school are missing of course. Meet Tumble Cottage's old owners." The sound of Mum's voice as she studied the photograph over my shoulder made me jump.

"I'm sorry darling. I didn't mean to scare you," she laughed, hugging me. "I bet you a week's pocket money the splendid fellow at the back is the old colonel Mrs P was wittering on about. He looks fierce enough to be Monty's second in command, don't you think?"

"His wife looks beautiful doesn't she Mum? The boy looks a bit, you know." I scrunched up my face.

"Uncool," laughed Mum. "Come on Alex. Be fair. Grey shorts and V-neck jumpers were the fashion in those days. The poor chap couldn't get Nike trainers, or fancy track suit bottoms in the 1940s you know."

I laughed back. "Do you think the baby was a girl or a boy."

"Not a clue Sooty," said Mum, stroking my arm as she used her pet name for me. "If the photo had been in colour we would have known for sure. Folk in those days were very traditional – pink for a girl, blue for a boy. But I guess that one will remain a mystery. Come on let's go in. It's getting dark."

CHAPTER 8

Jamie got excited over the Second World War soldier's helmet and waterbottle for all of five minutes before ditching them in favour of new millennium technology: a new game he had bought out of his pocket money for the PC called Alien Paranoia.

Corker's reaction was more unexpected. She didn't make any fuss when I told her about the tins we wouldn't be able to play shops with and exhibited only luke-warm interest in the old plates and forks and knives.

When Mum showed her the old photograph her behaviour was stranger still. One thing Corker loves is photographs. She pores over every snapshot we have ever taken of the family and loves to study the physical changes recorded in the albums as she and her brother and sister change with the years. Photos of babies, anyone's babies, are a particular favourite. They are usually examined avidly by Corker, along with an accompanying bombardment of questions concerning their pedigree: names, age, weight, sister's names, where they live, and so on.

But one glimpse of the old sepia-toned photograph was enough for Corker and when Mum offered it to her for closer inspection she drew back putting her hands down firmly by her sides. "It looks dirty, like spiders have been crawling on it," she said, sliding behind me to avoid any possibility of contact.

"It's only because it's been in the tea chest a long time and it is very old. But there's nothing wrong with it Corker," said Mum, the worm of a frown creasing her brow.

"Oh, let's forget it," said Dad. "Anyway, the soldier looks a grumpy old gimmer doesn't he Corker. That's the problem Mummy. It's nothing to worry about sweetheart. Mummy's going to put the picture away now anyway."

"On the bonfire? asked Corker hopefully.

"Well I think that would be a bit extreme," laughed Dad. "It's interesting because it shows the history of the house and another family who used to live here."

"In the loft," said Mum. "We'll put it in the loft with all the other old stuff so you won't have to ever look at it again if it bothers you that much."

Next day, Saturday, dawned cold and bright again, with a hint of snow in the air. The three of us had planned to go sledging at Tumblewood Hill, which was really no more than a series of playing fields at the end of our road. But we were in for a disappointment. The Hill was so popular for sledging that the snow had been worn away until it shone like bone in the steepest section, while the rest of the run had deteriorated into a swamp of brown slush and mud with bare patches of grass poking through. As we trudged disconsolately back home, wondering how we would spend the rest of that endless Saturday morning, Corker spotted the house.

"What in heavens name is that supposed to be. What kind of tramp lives in that house?" she scoffed in her most censorious voice.

Both Jamie and I scolded her for her rudeness, mainly because we were afraid anyone in the house might hear.

But Corker was right. The place looked a mess and appeared deserted. At least that was the impression from the outside. The hedge on the front garden wall was so overgrown that people had to walk by on the edge of the pavement. What could be glimpsed of the garden through the thick privet revealed a jungle of waist-high grass and weeds that the snow failed to cover. It was decorated with a liberal sprinkling of Coke and Sprite cans the local schoolchildren had no doubt lobbed over as their idea of a joke.

The driveway running up to the garage was littered with contents normally found *inside* a house. There was a plastic table, a couple of chairs, an old sofa – missing all its cushions, and charred and blackened as if someone had tried to set it alight, a washing machine, and a rusting aluminium kitchen sink.

The pathway leading up to the house was clear of domestic appliances, but weeds sprouted between the crazy paving and the porch and front door were almost obscured by the foliage of overhanging trees and bushes.

The lace on every window had long since turned from pearl white to dingy grey and every curtain was drawn tight shut. Although the house looked neglected and desolate, if anyone still lived there they clearly did not want visitors.

"Come on, the place gives me the creeps, let's get home," I said in my most commanding big sister voice. Jamie didn't need any second bidding. Tugging the string on the sledge he was moving away when Corker piped up. "There's milk bottles on the step. See just by the side of the door, Alex. They're full. Somebody *must live* there," my very smart little sister whispered, clearly awestruck at the idea of any human inhabiting such a ramshackle dwelling.

Silently cursing Corker's Sherlock Holmes' powers of deduction, I grabbed her hand and was pulling her wailing out of the driveway when the front door opened.

All protests ceased as Corker shot down beside me behind the wall. On the other side of the driveway, Jamie made a similar vanishing act as he stared in wide-eyed puzzlement at our behaviour. Putting my finger to my lips, I sneaked a look through a small gap between the wall and hedge – and felt the hair on the back of my neck prickle.

The small muffled figure I saw on the doorstep was the apparition I had seen on the road in the middle of the night.

It hadn't been my imagination. The creature existed and, worse, lived along the road from us. "Alex, you're hurting my hand," moaned Corker. "Sshhh," I warned releasing a grip that had subconsciously become vice-like on her fingers. "I can't see. Who is it? What's happening?"

"Quiet," I instructed, guiding her head alongside mine. "Just watch and be still."

So we watched as the character, dressed in the same long coat and wearing the scarf and hat I remembered in such vivid detail from my nocturnal sighting under the lamplight, emerged onto the porch.

In the small shambling steps I recalled so clearly, it (I still had no idea whether it was male or female) tottered to the milk bottles, pausing mid-way to wipe its nose with the back of a gloved hand.

"Yuk. Skankie," said Corker in disgust. "Be quiet," I hissed. But it was too late. Its head came up like the Robyn I had seen in our back garden. Alert. Enquiring. On guard. Listening for the slightest sound.

Thrashing my arms in silent mime, I waved my brother and sister down. "Statues. Be statues", I mouthed. After what seemed like an eternity the figure bent with painstaking slowness, picked up the milk bottles, and disappeared back inside the house.

Chapter 9

Later we held a summit conference in the twins' room with Jamie's sock drawer jamming the door closed and Corker's hand-made Do Not Disturb sign firmly in place as further deterrence against uninvited adults. After I had recounted every detail of my late night encounter with Skankie (a name we all agreed was fittingly shivery) twice over at Corker's insistence, we decided upon a plan of action.

Despite our terror of the mysterious figure, we resolved to find out more about it for one simple reason. It lived too close for comfort and, as Jamie said, placing his baseball bat carefully under his bed, it was better to find out the truth about our neighbour rather than lie awake every night imagining the horrible possibilities.

So I sneaked downstairs for some straws, cut them into different sizes in the bathroom with the scissors Dad used for his nose-hairs, and returned to the twins' bedroom with them peeking in an even line above my fist.

"Okay, here are the rules," I said. "Each of us will take it in turn to draw a straw and whoever picks the shortest one has to do the dare."

"Wait a minute!" exclaimed Jamie. "This is a fix. You know which straw is the shortest, so you're bound to win Alex."

"Duh. Think again Jamie," I said pouring as much scorn into my voice as is humanly possible for a 13 and a half year old – and that's a lot. "You and Corker will take your turns before me, so there's no way I can cheat, dummy."

Jamie was about to whack me with his plastic Roman's sword when Corker froze proceedings with the sixty-four-thousand dollar question.

"Dare, Alex? What's a dare?"

"A dare is something that no normal person would want to do, but (I went on quickly) it takes a lot of courage. In this case – a huge amount."

Jamie, cross-legged on the carpet, started moving restlessly from bum cheek to bum cheek. And Corker was sitting with her hand under her chin. Both sure signs that the natives were restless and about to scupper my idea with further questions. I had to move fast in order to stop any more thinking.

"Right Jamie. You go first," I said thrusting my fist with the three straws in front of his face. He eyed them like a condemned man facing the gallows. "Why not Corker," he whimpered.

"Oh for heaven's sake Jamie. Hurry up!"

In a huff, his arm shot out and he snatched the middle straw turning his back and retreating into the corner to study it.

Corker strode forward next. Her hazel eyes sparkled with the challenge and excitement of an unknown adventure. Her small hand came forward hovering over the right-hand straw. Then she hesitated, an invisible light bulb switching on above her head, she smiled in triumph. "Eenie, meanie, minie, mow. Catch a baby by the toe, If it squeals let it go, Eenie, meanie, minie, mow."

Her finger was pointing at the right straw on the last word of the rhyme and – with an exultant "yeeesss", she plucked it making her own victory fist.

"Everyone, show your straws now," I commanded.

Reluctantly, Jamie turned and showed his straw. I produced mine, and Corker's hand shot out with hers. Corker's was shortest by a good inch.

CHAPTER 10

Even though Corker had drawn the shortest straw, none of us slept very well that night. Sunday morning, exactly one week and one day before Christmas Day, dawned with what Dad called a Moscow sky – red and threatening. By the time we finished a hurried breakfast the first few, solitary snowflakes were fluttering on to the patio. These turned out to be the advance guard sent ahead to scout out the lie of the land. The main force of this white army – a million thick, brilliant white parachutes - came tumbling down in an endless stream to commence the barrage in earnest as we got into our coats.

"Wow. Look at that. It's pelting down. We'll get soaked," yelled Jamie, skipping with glee as Mum pulled up the hood on Corker's duffel coat and double-wrapped her own long blue scarf around her neck."

"Now listen, try and not get too wet," said Mum with a sigh, knowing that she was asking the impossible.

"Alex, you're in charge. Twins' you listen to your big sister, do as she says, and stay beside her. Make sure you go on the sledge with Corker, Alex. All of you keep your gloves on - and the minute any of you feel too cold come straight back."

But Mum was talking to herself. We were already running half way down the drive pulling our decoy, the sledge, behind us.

I felt guilty over lying to Mum about the true nature of our expedition. It was literally a white lie I thought as I looked at my coat already covered in a shroud of snow.

Thump! A large wet snowball exploded on my neck sending a stream of ice-cold powder down my back. "Direct hit," shouted Jamie as he dissolved into his trademark hyena laugh. "Race you to the hill Alex. Last one there's a monkey's bum." His mad cackle echoed in the trees as he ran through the swirling storm.

I ran after him catching the hood of his anorak and tugging him back hard. He fell with a satisfyingly wet plop on the snow and as he stared innocently up at me through wide blue eyes a big flake landed on a long lash and he blinked and laughed with wonder.

My anger melted. I could never stay angry long at my silly little brother's antics, but I forced myself to stifle the smile and maintain my seriously ticked-off big sister expression.

"Jamie. Cut the nonsense out now," I shouted, pulling him to his feet and shaking the snow from his clothes. "In case you've forgotten, we're not here to go sledging. We have to find out more about Skankie. You said so yourself last night, remember?"

He nodded reluctantly and we trudged on in silence until we got to the house.

The snowstorm made the place look even more neglected. The driveway leading to the garage was already covered, and the abandoned furniture seemed even more forlorn under its white blanket.

Peeping through the hedge up the path the only disturbance we could see were the tiny tracks of a bird and the print of some small four-legged creature. There was no sign of a human, or Skankie-type footprint in the fresh snow. The front door looked resolutely shut, and the curtains on every window remained the same as the day before – tightly drawn against the encroaching gaze of the outside world.

Well, almost every one was tightly drawn. After five minutes of trance-like staring through the hypnotic blizzard, I noticed that the curtain on a window at the side of the house nearest the garage was open the tiniest sliver. Perfect.

"Right Corker. Battle stations," I said briskly in a bid to disguise the rising tide of nerves. I pointed out the target window. "It's our best chance of seeing anything. You can use the furniture in the driveway as cover."

Somehow, the look of devil-may-care adventure had deserted Corker overnight. "I don't know Alex. I'm cold," she whimpered.

"Look, a dare's a dare. Right? Nobody goes back on a dare. It's like (I hesitated for a moment trying to imagine the worst offence possible) It's like weeing the bed at night and then not telling anybody about it."

"Ugh Skankie." Corker made a disgusted face.

"Exactly," I said pushing on. "We drew the straws last night. It was fair. We'll be right here behind you. Nothing can happen. Let's get it done."

I copied Corker's triumphant "yeess" and followed up with her trade-mark air punch.

Her face set in the grim lines of a junior commando, Corker moved clear of the hedge. She went up the driveway in a spider crouch, pink Pocahontas gumboots moving as fast as the thickening snow would allow. Half way up she ducked behind the washing machine and looked back. Jamie and I both gave forced smiles and a hesitant thumbs-up. Then she dodged past the chairs and hunkered down behind the table.

"Deep breaths," I mouthed at her. "Take deep breaths." She nodded in-haling and exhaling in huge exaggerated gulps of air.

Thirty seconds later she was up again and heading for the sanctuary of the burnt-out sofa – the last piece of cover between the driveway and the window.

There she sat for almost a minute without looking back. This time Jamie and I held our breath. Had our brave little sister had enough? Was she about to throw in the towel?

We should have known better. With a final wave to us, she was up again and darting the final few feet over no-man's land to the window.

Beside me Jamie was jumping up and down silently cheering his twin sister's performance – a sight rarely seen in our household believe me. "Top girl Corker," I whispered in exultation. "Now for the last bit and home."

Slowly, like a snake uncoiling from a basket, our sister unwound to her full height of four feet and three inches and applied her unlazy eye to the tiny slit in the lace curtain.

For a second, as her sight adjusted from the dazzling brilliance of the falling snow, she could see nothing inside but blackness. Suddenly from out of the darkness another eye – a monstrous red bloodshot eye bulging with veins – loomed on the other side of the pane and stared unblinking into her beautiful hazel eye.

Screaming like a banshee, Corker charged headlong back down the driveway. Whereas on the outward journey the furniture offered valuable hiding places, on the panic-stricken return it now represented a dangerous obstacle course. She fell over a plastic chair and collapsed on the sofa in her desperate retreat. By the time Corker reached us she was minus a pink gumboot, covered in snow, and weeping hysterically.

"A monster," she gasped between sobs. "Skankie's a huge red-eyed monster Alex."

Like a cold, panic is infectious and I started to shake as I grabbed my little sister's hand. We had to get away immediately before the huge, slavering red-eyed monster came crashing through the front door and lumbered down the path to devour us like so much lumpy custard.

The same kind of nightmares must have been racing through Jamie's head too because he was moaning with fright as he twisted the sledge string repeatedly through his fingers. But Corker's bravery must have rubbed off on him because Jamie sprinted back up Skankie's driveway and scooped up the gumboot. Waving the piece of pink rubber above his head like a war trophy, he screamed at the top of his lungs – "run for your lives" – before tossing it to me as he came rushing past us.

Pausing only to jam the boot back on to the wailing Corker's soaking foot, we took Jamie's advice and followed his rapidly receding figure sprinting pell-mell through the snow-storm. After what seemed like a marathon race, we collapsed in an exhausted heap together. Breath coming in ragged gasps, legs aching from the exertion of our flight, we turned and stared back through the blizzard searching for the chasing monster until our eyes hurt. Mercifully it failed to materialise and, by degrees our jangled nerves calmed down, and we began taking in our surroundings.

It quickly became apparent that we had not run 26 miles, but a mere 400 yards, and were no further from Skankie's house of horrors than the playing fields at the end of the road. But we had entered a different world. There were lots of other children here and most of them looked like they were having the time of their lives. The morning's snowfall had transformed Tumblewood Hill from a threadbare patch of ice and mud to a sledging paradise and children of all shapes and sizes on all kinds of sledges, ranging from trays to high-tech toboggans, were taking full advantage of the conditions.

Jamie was first to catch the bug. Pulling our plastic sledge to the edge of the steepest section, he belly-flopped onto it, and using his arms like flippers, disappeared over the precipice. "Yahoo!" The disembodied shriek of pure pleasure drifted up to us seconds later followed – after a considerably longer period – by Jamie himself, grinning from ear to ear, and giving a very good impersonation of the Abominable Snowman.

"It's wicked. Come on Alex, Corker, try it." One look at Corker's pinched, pale face told me she was still suffering from the aftershock of our earlier adventure. But I also knew that a good dose of fun was the best way of helping her forget the frightening memories.

"Come on Corker," I said. "You go in front and I'll get on behind you so you don't fall off." She whimpered about her wet sock and cold hands and wanting to see Mum. Gradually, I coaxed her to the top of the run for a look. Then she reluctantly agreed to try it once. After that, Jamie and I finally managed to drag her away from Tumblewood Hill two hours later.

CHAPTER 11

We had to pass Skankie's house again on the way home. But we resolved to give it the widest berth possible by running past as fast as we could on the other side of the road.

Everything would have been fine, and I believe the things we saw later that Christmas wouldn't have happened, at least not to us, if we had only ignored the moaning and kept running.

Instead Jamie stopped and looked at me with the same silent appeal he had used on Dad when he was driving the car and knocked down a fox in Yorkshire.

Despite the fact that he is only seven, Jamie has an astonishing, some would say irritating, sense of fairness and compassion for all living things. Even the little horrors in the rugby team, who won't pass to him. So the pitiful cry of someone clearly in pain was bound to halt Jamie in his tracks – even though the sound came from Skankie's house.

Corker simply stood rooted to the spot and refused to move an inch towards the house. But Jamie was adamant about the need to investigate and – although I was little keener than Corker – I forced myself to go with him.

Leaving strict instructions for Corker that she should run as fast as she could and get Dad if we were not back out within five minutes, we crept over the road towards Skankie's house.

As we drew nearer to the hedge the moaning grew appreciably louder. I flinched at the sound and hesitated, but the distressing nature of the sound spurred Jamie on. He peered through the hedge, gasped, and then without a backward glance, ran up the path.

Cursing my little brother's caring nature, I ran after him.

The scene that met my eyes as I turned the corner of the hedge replaced my fear with concern. The horrifying creature we called Skankie was lying at a broken angle between the top step and the porch amidst a sea of dairy cream and smashed glass. It was clear that any red-eyed monster had been the product of our fevered imaginations. Skankie was no more than a feeble old man, who had fallen in the snow while attempting to pick up his milk. Jamie was already kneeling beside the man, whose hat was tilted at a drunken angle on his head. His scarf remained wrapped around his face, and he was groaning weakly from behind it. As I reached the man he was pointing with a gloved hand at the bottles as if to warn us about the glass.

Two sensations struck me straight away. The overpowering odour that came from Skankie was not simply the cold greasy smell of someone who badly needed a wash. There was also another smell that no amount of bathing could cure: the underlying stench of decay, which seemed to seep from every pore. Skankie. By luck, or intuition, we had chosen exactly the right name for him.

Close up, like a digitally enhanced picture, I saw the curdled mixture of blood, milk and glass splinters on the icy doorstep and I felt the back of my neck grow hot and a dizzying wave of nausea hit me. But I forced back the sickness and made myself listen to what Skankie was trying to say.

"...leg. It's just my knee son. I'll be all right. Just help me up." With the combined assistance of Jamie and I, the old man managed to lever himself back on to his feet. Supporting his shaking arms, I realised that the source of my abject terror was no more than a bag of bones. A trouser leg was flapping at the knee and through the tear I noticed a nasty gash about an inch long.

"Maybe you should go to the hospital," I said. "I'll get my Dad to phone for an ambulance."

The old man shook his head vehemently. "No. No. There's no need to go putting anyone to any trouble. It's only a cut. I've had worse. I'll be fine once I get back inside. Just help me to the door children."

His voice still quavered from the shock of the fall and he was old and infirm. But the decision had the unmistakable firmness of an adult. Shrugging my shoulders at Jamie, I signalled for him to take a side and we steered Skankie across the porch. As I took his arm again, his coat sleeve rode up and for a second I glimpsed blackened and scarred flesh. My stomach did a long, slow roll and I could feel the gorge rising once more. Then he was brushing my hand aside and muttering goodbye from behind his scarf as he closed the door on us.

Chapter 12

We were not to know it, but that final week before Christmas proved to be the most momentous of our lives. It began, as most things do, with the best of intentions.

Having dispelled our fears that Skankie was a monster, Jamie set the ball rolling by calling another summit conference to suggest that we do something to help our neighbour in what was after all the season of goodwill.

Corker was still wary, but she came round quickly when we started discussing practical methods of assistance. We agreed that, given the state of the outside of the house and his obvious failure to wash, he must live alone. So we would volunteer to do errands for Skankie, like the shopping, getting his newspaper - "and sweeping the snow off his doorstep so he doesn't fall over again" - Corker chipped in enthusiastically.

Feeling proud, and justifiably satisfied with ourselves for such a brilliant idea, we marched around to Skankie's house that Monday morning to inform the old man of our decision.

At first we didn't think the rusty old bell could be working as Corker virtually leaned on it for five minutes without any sign of movement in the house. Then, just as we were turning to leave, we heard shuffling steps and the creak and rattle of bolts and chains being drawn. The front door opened a crack and Skankie's muffled features peered out.

"Yes. What do you want?" he asked in a not entirely friendly voice. Completely missing the tone, Corker launched into an explanation of our brilliant idea. Skankie stopped her in full, breathless flow.

"Shopping? I do my own shopping. Have done for years, long before you arrived in this street. Newspaper? Never buy one. There's nothing in the news these days. I have all the newspapers I need from the old days. Things happened then. Lots of things long before any of you were thought of."

His eyes took on a far off, dreamy quality and he stared through the three of us as if we were invisible. "Children. I used to have children long ago, long gone. I look for them though. I haven't given up. I look for them all the time."

Then the moment passed, his vision cleared, and he became aware of us again. "Thank you. I didn't thank you properly for helping me yesterday," he said in a more gentle voice. All of you were very kind."

An expression of regret came into his eyes as he looked at Corker. "Children. I know children like sweets. I don't have any I'm afraid. I'll get some when I'm next at the shops. I'll write it down, so I don't forget. Tell me your names."

I blushed. "No, that's all right. We didn't come here for sweets. Only to help and see how you are. I hope you're knee's okay."

He looked down at his leg and as he did so a shaggy ball of grey fur with white streaks and brilliant yellow eyes darted past him and down the path. "Oh no. Noodles!" he cried. "Stop. Come back." The old man shuffled on to the porch waving his arm at the cat as it disappeared through the gate. As he did so, the front door swung open and a familiar stench greeted my nostrils. Cats! It would have taken far more than the vanishing Noodles to create such an overwhelming stink. Skankie and Mrs P clearly had a common love of the creatures. I knew the mess my parents had been left to clear up in the cats' room at Tumble Cottage. So I shuddered at the thought of the state of Skankie's house if the frail old man allowed a tribe of felines the run of the place.

A glimpse at the dark interior of the hall confirmed my suspicions. Bundles of old newspapers were stacked against every wall, in some places up to a height of around five feet. Fighting for space between the papers was an ageing umbrella stand, containing what appeared to be parts of a car engine, and a grandfather clock with a cracked face that looked as though it had stopped ticking a long time ago. In a corner over from the clock stood a bath on fancy wrought iron legs. It was impossible to say whether the bath would have looked more ridiculous in the hall, or on the garage drive. But I had the feeling it had been making its way outside for some years. Hanging at a lop-sided angle on the wall above the bath lay a shelf groaning with an assortment of bric-a-brac that would have been more at home in a junk shop. There was a row of flying duck ornaments, resting on their sides rather than flying up the wall, a mug featuring a much younger version of the Queen's face, a chipped green vase sprouting plastic flowers, and right at the end a small light blue cross attached to a faded dark blue and gold ribbon. It reminded me of the medal my Mum once won for running a marathon.

The phrase "bull in a China shop" ran through my head for no logical reason, although I guessed a bull couldn't have made more mess if it had been set loose in Skankie's house.

The old man must have read my thoughts. When he saw me staring into his home, he appeared embarrassed, shuffling as quickly as his legs would allow him to close the door again.

Of course, we could never have guessed but – though we would see Noodles again in spine-chilling circumstances - that was the last time we saw Skankie, at least in his home.

Chapter 13

The accident happened the following night. The terrifying screech of brakes, followed by a bang like a thunderclap, would have wakened the dead. Even so, we were slow to clear the sleep from our senses and by the time we assembled at the front door Mum and Dad were already outside.

It looked like a scene from "Casualty", and I had to pinch myself to make sure I wasn't still upstairs in bed dreaming. But the whirring blue lights of the ambulance and police car seemed real enough. A policeman was speaking urgently into his radio, while Mum and Dad hovered anxiously near the ambulance.

A big black jeep was at the bottom of our drive buried in one of the pine trees at what seemed like an impossible angle. Its rear wheels were in mid air, spinning slowly, as if it was still attempting to go somewhere. But the once sleek, shiny bonnet was now a mangled heap of metal leaking steam and oil in a mist of boiling vapour. For a second, through the curtain of steam, I saw the shape of a body slumped in the front seat. It looked too small to be the driver.

Then my line of sight was blocked as another policeman and a paramedic, dressed in green overalls, advanced on the wreck. There was the protest of twisted metal as the paramedic attempted to open the passenger door. It failed to budge and the policeman lifted his truncheon and smashed the glass. The man in green overalls leaned through the window towards the figure. A minute later his head re-emerged and he shook it slowly once. An ominous groan, followed by the crack of breaking wood, sent the men scrambling for cover as the tree collapsed flattening the car like a crushed can in a storm of dust and branches.

In the silence that followed I became aware of movement beyond the crash scene. As my eyes became accustomed to the blackness, I saw another paramedic leaning over something in the road. It was too far to distinguish what the shape was.

Like sleep walking, my legs propelled me further down the garden without me being fully conscious I was moving. Somehow I knew what had happened and what I would find on the road.

"Alex. Alex. Don't leave us. Where are you going?" Corker's plea snapped me out of the trance. She was weeping and Jamie stood with his thumb jammed into his mouth staring after me.

As I turned back to them, I heard the stern voice of the policeman with the radio. "Hey kids. Come on. This is no place for you. Get back inside right now."

Mum and Dad, who had been equally oblivious to our presence, moved quickly over to us.

"Come on," said Dad, putting his arm around my shoulder and steering me towards the house. "There's been a terrible accident, but it's over. There's nothing we can do."

As our parents shepherded us back indoors, I turned once more in time to see the paramedics load the stretcher on to the ambulance. As they opened the back doors, the sheet covering the body slipped and a limp gloved hand fell down. I didn't need to ask Dad who it was. I knew the frail old man we called Skankie had been hit by the car and wept at the thought.

Chapter 14

The hospital had the longest, straightest corridors I had ever seen. The floors smelled of disinfectant and were covered in green linoleum, shiny with age and the constant flow of human traffic. White-coated doctors with clipboards and stethoscopes rushed along them. Old people in pyjamas and slippers shuffled zimmers in the slow lane, occasionally overtaken by porters pushing patients in wheelchairs, or tea ladies pushing sandwich trolleys. We went in single file, picking our way through the throng behind Mum towards a set of swing doors with a sign above which read Intensive Care Unit.

Mum hadn't said much on the car journey to the hospital. The night before she had listened patiently as we made our case for visiting Skankie. The old man lived alone and probably wouldn't have anyone to visit him, we pleaded. He might need plants watered at home and, after all, we were his neighbours. As a last desperate resort we had even thrown in Noodles. There wouldn't be anyone to look after his cat. Noodles would starve if he wasn't fed. The old man could give us instructions.

None of our arguments impressed Mum one bit. All of us knew that, before she trotted out her favourite saying: "Do you lot think your Dad and I came down the Clyde in a banana boat?"

We never had a clue what Mum was talking about whenever she referred to the Clyde and banana boats. But we knew we had won when she smiled at the Noodles ruse. Although she stressed - it was against her "better judgment" – Mum relented and agreed to take us on a brief visit to see Skankie, providing the hospital permitted it.

Since we didn't know his real name – and Mum could hardly ask for Mr Skankie – she gave the accident details to a clerk at the big reception desk in the main entrance. He made a phone call and then told Mum that Mr Robert Thomson was on "the critical list" and visitors were not allowed.

Mr Robert Thomson. So that was Skankie's name – a pretty normal sounding one for a red-eyed monster, I thought. And suddenly I felt my lip trembling and on the verge of tears. "What's the critical list Mum?" I asked, already half knowing and dreading the answer. "It's when somebody is very ill Alex," she said. "Like, they could die?" I said, and this time I couldn't stop the tears streaming down my face. Mum shifted uncomfortably and taking my hand, motioned the twins' to follow us out.

"Wait a moment," said the clerk. He picked up the phone again and spoke quietly into it before waving us over. "I've had a word with the Ward Sister," he told Mum. "She has no objection to you coming up for a quick visit. But Mr Thomson has been unconscious since he was brought in. He's on a ventilator. He won't be aware of anyone."

"You heard that children," said Mum. "Sk…, sorry Mr Thomson won't know you're visiting him. Do you still want to see him?"

We nodded solemnly and Corker said: "God will tell him," which made Mum blink quickly a couple of times and pinch her nose.

As we approached the double doors with the ominous sign above it, I began to wonder if this really was such a good idea. But Corker was forging ahead now, pulling Mum's hand and we were through before I could voice any second thoughts.

After the bustle of the main corridors, the Intensive Care Unit was a haven of peace. So pin-drop quiet that the squeak of the Ward Sister's rubber shoes sounded ear-splittingly loud, like chalk being scratched across a blackboard, as she crossed the floor from her office to meet us.

She was small, round and rosy-cheeked with a face that looked as if it laughed a lot. But today her features were set and grim as she guided us down a narrow corridor to a room with a large window instead of a wall.

Gazing through the window we saw a bed surrounded by a battery of machines and tubes. "What do all those squiggly lines mean?" asked Corker, pointing at the screens of the machines.

"Well dear, the green lines show us what Mr Thomson's brain is doing," said the nurse patting Corker's head. "And the red lines show us what his heart is doing."

"How are they doing?"

"They're doing all right at the moment sweetheart. If they weren't the green line would go all jaggy, and the hilly red line would go flat and straight. But you must remember that Mr Thomson is old and very ill. That's why these machines have to monitor his condition."

Our gaze shifted beyond the machines and tubes to the condition of the patient. Looking tiny in the centre of the bed was Skankie, or at least his head. The rest of his body was encased in sheets, but for the first time we saw the old man's face exposed without the covering hat or scarf. And what we saw made me gasp.

Skankie's head looked like an ancient tortoise that had been baked in a micro-wave oven for too long. His face was a mass of hideous scars and burns of horrifying shades, fried brown in some places, crisped black in others. Where a nose should have been, there was simply a hole. His lips looked as if they had melted and been remoulded in plastic, while the flesh around the old man's eyes was drawn down tight in two large, angry red circles that looked as if they wept. Thankfully his eyes were closed. What was left of his hair was a wispy brown curl or two fighting for survival on a skull that was otherwise a charred crater.

"What on earth happened to him?" I whispered, at once horrified and fascinated by the monstrous sight. "Your friend was terribly badly burned in a fire once. We don't know the circumstances, but we found the scars all over his body. Quite honestly, I don't know how he survived. It must have been a miracle. But over the years he hasn't received the proper follow-up treatment and all sorts of problems were setting in even before he had the accident."

"What about relatives?" asked Mum. The nurse shook her head. "All we know is what social services have told us. According to their records, Mr Thomson has lived alone for a long time. Apparently he was married, but his wife died several years ago. He had a son but he died tragically at a young age. He also had a daughter, but social services say there is no trace of her. Anyway, judging from Mr Thomson's age, if she's still alive, she would be an elderly lady now. So he might well be alone in the world. It was kind of you children to think of him."

Chapter 15

Like us, Mum and Dad regularly had their own summit conferences, where children were strictly forbidden. They held one in the big lounge that night, while we attempted to eavesdrop pressed up against the keyhole next door in the little lounge. The covering noise of the TV reduced their conversation to obscure murmurs.

Jamie reckoned he had hit on the solution when he remembered a scene from a spy movie. Sprinting to the kitchen he was back in record time with a tumbler. Applying one end of the glass to the door and the other to his ear, he listened intently for several minutes until I grabbed it from him. "You're listening through the wrong end dummy, it's the drinking end that goes against the door, not the bottom."

As it turned out neither end worked – I still could only hear a jumbled murmur through the glass – and Jamie was forced to conclude that the surveillance methods employed in spy movies were maybe not everything they were cracked up to be after all.

Either way, we didn't have long to wait to discover the subject matter of our parents' top- secret pow- wow.

Mum chose bedtime, when she was brushing our teeth and we couldn't answer back (she's fiendishly ingenious is our Mum), to inform us that we wouldn't be returning to the hospital again.

"As the nurse said, it was very kind of you all to think about Mr Thomson," she said, working the electric toothbrush in tiny circles around

Corker's molars. "But, if you are honest, I'm sure you'll all agree that the visit was far too upsetting."

"Nnnmmmm." Corker spluttered her violent disagreement, almost choking on the brush, as pink and white spray went up her nose and down her chin.

Since Jamie and I were similarly preoccupied – and had to spit down the sink first before we could argue – the battle was effectively over before any of us could say anything understandable."

"I won't hear another word," said Mum. "He's not a relative. Why we hardly even know Mr Thomson. As virtual strangers, it would be an intrusion if we went again."

"We cleaned his path. He's kind," screeched Corker. "That's enough Kristie," said Mum employing my little sister's Sunday-best name in a tone that would accept no further argument. "The subject is closed and I don't want to hear about it again. You can pray for Mr Thomson to get well soon. But now it's time for bed and a quiet time."

Surprisingly, that night none of us had nightmares about poor Skankie's horrible face. Jamie and Corker seemed to sleep soundly beneath their half-moon night- light. But I did have a dream and, though like most dreams it was all jumbled and didn't make any sense, it was bad.

It was night and I found myself outside in my pyjamas with one of Mum's old marathon medals around my neck. I was standing in a large open space. The place seemed familiar, and I felt I should know it. But somehow it wasn't quite right, as if things were both missing and at the same time present in the place which altered it completely. I could only sense these changes because – although I could feel the coolness of evening air on my face – it was pitch black.

Then I looked up and, despite the fact that it was still coal black night, I saw a giant shadow directly overhead. For what must only have been a heart-beat in time the shadow eclipsed every sense in my body. I could not see, or hear, and the shadow dropped down like a blanket, first smothering and then consuming me. My lungs were on fire with an unbearable heat, and the dark-ness was tomb-like. Then Mum's marathon medal started to glow around my neck and when I looked up again the shadow had been replaced by a searing light, which exploded in a tower of orange flames.

I woke up in a cold sweat and a tangle of covers. At first I thought the screams were a remnant of my dreams and lay still trying to calm my pounding heart. Gradually though, I realised they were real and coming from outside. They came suddenly, rending the silence of the night in short, sharp staccato bursts at a decibel level which was screeching pitch. They sounded like creatures being tortured.

I resolved there and then that there would be no repeat of my frightening night sighting of Skankie. The screams were coming from outside. Inside was safe. Bed was safer still, particularly when your head was under the covers. Diving beneath the duvet, I stuck my fingers in my ears and, humming loudly to myself, began counting slowly to twenty.

At 15, the screams came again, jolting me out of my snug cocoon like a cold shower. Investigation, or a sleepless night? I knew the answer before the follow-up screeching sent another shiver down my spine. Okay, here were the rules. There would be no trip outside. In fact there would be no venturing beyond the bedroom. The window was the limit, and if I couldn't solve the mystery then, Mum and Dad would have to be wakened up, though that was the last resort.

Still shivering from the nightmare, I wrapped the duvet around my shoulders and sneaked over to the window. Peeping over the sill, I stared into the back garden expecting to see a pack of goblins ripping each other apart. At first I could see nothing, but then there was a flurry of movement on the patio directly under my window and another screech. Cats. The sound was no more than some cats fighting. "Yaaaagh. Clear off," I yelled, knocking on my window as the furry shapes darted into the night. A guilty thought struck me as I returned to bed. What if one of the cats had been poor Noodles? I really should have gone outside to investigate I decided as I fell into a mercifully dreamless sleep.

CHAPTER 16

"Wakey, wakey. Rise and shine. Breakfast's ready." Mum didn't need to tell us. The glorious aroma of bacon and eggs had been wafting upstairs for the past ten minutes and our stomachs were growling in anticipation of our favourite Saturday morning fry-up.

"The countdown's well and truly on now kids," welcomed Mum as we catapulted into the kitchen. "Only eight days until Christmas and it looks like Santa will have to hire a snowmobile to make his deliveries this year." I gazed out on the scene. In the driveway our people carrier had been transformed into a white shapeless box and the scars from the accident – including the shattered pine – had been obliterated by the overnight fall.

"Wowee," yelled Jamie, devouring his breakfast at warp factor speed. "Let's get out in the garden and make a snowman."

"Carrot and buttons Mum," I shouted, immediately warming to the project.

"And coal for the eyes, remember," piped up Corker from the chair she was standing on to unveil the latest date in the Advent calendar.

Our snowman went exceptionally well that day. The snow was exactly right for rolling large balls. Not too powdery, not too slushy, or icy. But thick and sticking together so well that we managed to roll a huge body in one go, while Dad helped to plonk an impressive head on top. It was while Mum was adding the finishing touches with one of her old hats and a scarf that I noticed the food was still there.

"Look Mum, the foxes haven't touched the food we left out," I said pointing to the bag that remained intact hanging from our usual branch.

"That's odd," she said, after examining the bag to make sure the Reynard family hadn't managed to spirit the pizza left-overs away in a method other than their normally extremely messy fashion. "It's so cold I thought they would have been delighted with a couple of slices of thick crust American Hot. Never mind Alex, I'm sure they'll be back again tomorrow, especially if the weather stays like this."

In fact we never saw Rat's Tail, or Youngblood again – though Old Mangy paid one final unexpected visit. It was early on a Saturday morning exactly one week before Christmas. Jamie had to get up early for rugby. Mum had taken his shirt off the wash line and she had left the back kitchen door open while she went through to the utility room to iron it.

Jamie was on his own in the kitchen at the table eating Frosties with his back to the door when – he told us later – the hair on the back of his neck suddenly prickled and he sensed that he was not alone.

He turned around slowly to see Old Mangy standing motionless inside the doorway. Jamie knew instinctively that if he made any sound the fox would bolt. Instead he sat perfectly still and waited as the creature stared at him. The fox continued to do so for what must have only been seconds, but seemed like several minutes: its eyes glittering with an almost human intelligence. Then it dropped something from its mouth. Jamie shielded his eyes as a tiny golden disc spun through the winter sunlight to land on the tiled floor with an echoing metallic tinkle. Jamie swore later that Old Mangy nodded as if to say: "Here I am, I've delivered the message. Now it's up to you humans to work it out." Then the spell was broken and the fox disappeared for the last time down the garden as Jamie moved from his chair.

What he found was a brass button that looked as though it had come from a military uniform. He showed it to Corker and I later that day. But we had no understanding of what it meant until the very end.

I can only guess that the Reynard family sensed what was coming and – given that they can up-sticks and find a new home a lot easier than humans – decided to get away from Tumble Cottage as fast as possible.

If only animals could talk they might have warned us. Or perhaps we could have read the signs better and been more prepared. Then again it was probably too late. I suspect the invisible engine responsible for such seemingly impossible events had already come to life and was growling, preparing to spring long before the foxes vanished. In any event, everything started to happen that night – six nights before Christmas.

Chapter 17

That was the night Corker heard the screaming cats. She wasn't awake in our normal understanding of the word. But she rose in her night dress as the first echoes were barely dying, put on her towelling robe and pink Barbie slippers under the yellow half-moon night light, and without hesitation went downstairs and unlocked the patio doors.

"Jamie. Jamie." Jamie tossed and turned in restless dreams as the insistent voice of his twin-sister called to him. "Jamie. It's cold. I need you here. Come quickly." Jamie drew his covers tighter and curled into a ball trying to drown out the inner voice. It began to work. She was fading away. Growing more distant.

The cats had scattered the instant Corker had opened the French Windows and gone out on to the patio. He could see her now. She was half way down the first section of the garden. But what was she doing outside in the snow in her dressing gown and slippers. Slippers! Her feet would get soaked. The slippers would be ruined. Mum would have a fit. Boy was she in for it! Jamie smiled in his sleep at the thought and drooled contentedly on to the pillow.

Corker was further down the first section of garden now. She had almost reached the semi-circle of fir trees. Crikey, the snow was deep even here under the trees. It was up to his sister's knees. How could she stand such cold, he wondered as he snoozed.

Wait a minute. What was that shimmering through the trees? Something blue. A blue coloured light flickering in the darkness beyond the fir trees.

Corker was going into the trees now. She was disappearing into the second section of garden. He couldn't see her anymore. "Jamie! Jamie!" Her voice suddenly clanged in his brain with the urgency of an alarm bell.

Unlike his sister, Jamie dived out of bed fully awake and, charging through my bedroom door, shook me roughly awake.

Pausing only to pull on our gum boots and coats, we rushed out into the night tracing the clear footprints of Corker through the middle of the garden.

We saw the shimmering blue light half way down the first section. It seemed to be coming from somewhere beyond the fir trees and appeared to weaken one second and grow stronger the next like a bulb on the point of blowing a fuse.

"It could be burglars," I said. "Let's get Mum and Dad."

"You do what you want. I'm getting Corker," said Jamie ploughing on without a backward glance at me. Ashamed at my cowardice, I stumbled through the drifts after Jamie.

We heard the crying as we emerged from the trees into the second section of the garden. At first I thought it was Corker and I wished I had picked up Mum's torch from the house as we peered desperately into the darkness.

"There she is!" said Jamie, pointing down the path of crazy paving. I saw her almost immediately. She was half way down the path with her back to us, standing completely immobile and staring, as if entranced, towards the right hand corner of the garden.

At the same moment, I realised that the crying we heard was not Corker. It was too high and keening for the sound any seven-year-old would make. Jamie's head turned slowly from the motionless figure of his twin sister and he looked at me. I couldn't see his face, but that didn't stop me knowing what his question would be before he voiced it. "Cats?" he asked, hoping my reply would confirm what he already knew was a lie. "No," I said, feeling my voice shaking from something more than the cold. "That's the sound of a baby crying."

We reached Corker at the same time. More than the light, it was my little sister's stillness that frightened me. She was like a petrified statue. In the numbing cold, not a muscle twitched, or an eye blinked through lashes that were already beginning to grow brittle under a sheen of frost. She simply stood staring at the clump of rhododendron bushes by the side of the garden. Or rather, she stared straight through the bushes as though hypnotised by the blue glow that shimmered with intermittent strength somewhere beyond them.

The crying, I realised, had quietened to sobs. But the insistent sound was still unmistakably that of a baby and it also seemed to come from beyond the bushes in the same direction as the blue light.

An involuntary shudder travelled up my spine. I didn't want to be here in the dead of night at the bottom of our garden seeing mysterious lights and hearing sounds that could not be possible. I wanted to be back in the warmth and safety of my bed. I wanted to run back to the house now, with or without my brother and sister.

"No. No. We mustn't go there Corker. The crash. It's not safe." Jamie's anguished cry shocked me into action. I saw him make a desperate grab for Corker just as she began to move down the path again. He missed and, arms flailing, fell into a drift. I ploughed on through the snow somehow knowing I had to catch Corker before she got beyond the holly bush. Imitating one of Jamie's spectacular rugby tackles, I threw myself full length catching Corker's back foot as she was taking the last step around the bushes.

We both fell in a swirl of glittering crystals and powder. At the last second, before my head went under the drift and I choked on a mouthful of snow, I glimpsed the blue light apparently suspended in mid-air and a shadow – the shadow of a woman – was captured in its flickering glow.

Then my mind focused on the little sister I was holding on to for dear life. Corker lay still in the snow. I touched her face. It was frozen. I lifted her arm and it flopped back down without protest. "Jamie! We've got to get Corker back inside right now!" I shouted, subconsciously realising that my voice was the only sound I now heard. Whoever, or whatever, had been in the garden was no longer there. The baby's sobs had vanished along with the shimmering blue light.

With me taking her legs and Jamie the arms, we somehow managed to lift Corker's limp body and struggle back to the house.

Inside, we laid her on the settee in the little lounge and removed her soaking slippers. Remembering my Brownie training, I sent Jamie for her duvet. "She's like ice," I said clasping her hand, while Jamie wrapped Corker's cats-in-pink-pyjamas duvet around her unconscious figure.

He sniffed loudly and then started to cry. "Alex, I'm scared. We should get Mum and Dad." Looking at the frightening stillness of my normally battery-charged little sister, I felt scared too.

But something made me pause. A small voice inside my head whispered insistently: "Wait. Just a little longer. Everything will be all right if you hold on."

"Jamie, stay with her, I'll be right back," I said. Running into the kitchen, I filled the electric kettle with water and then rummaged around in the cupboards searching for a hot water bottle. I found it just as the shrill whistle started to blow, signalling the water was boiling, and darted back to switch it off before the noise wakened Mum and Dad.

Wrapping the bottle in a towel, I placed it against Corker's back and ordered Jamie, who was sitting on the floor with his finger in his mouth, back into action. "Come on Jamie. We've got to get her awake. Rub her." I rubbed her arms and legs and then got Jamie to take over, while I gently slapped Corker's face.

"Aaargh! Stop. Stop. Leave me alone." The slapping did the trick. My fierce little sister opened her blue-ringed eyes and let out the sort of grumpy yell that proved she was very much back in the land of the living.

She flatly refused to let Jamie touch her. But, despite her vigorous protests, I kept rubbing her hands and feet until I felt the warmth creeping into them again.

"What's going on? What are you doing?" she complained as I frog marched her around the lounge. "Shh. You'll wake Mum and Dad," I warned."
Finally, satisfied that her blood was circulating properly again, I led her up to bed, while Jamie followed with the duvet and hot water bottle.

As we tucked her in, I nuzzled her ear with my nose and whispered. "Why were you in the garden Corker?"

"When?" she mumbled.

"Tonight," I said. "You were in the garden in the middle of the night in your slippers and dressing gown. Why Corks?

"Help," she sighed. "We've got to help them before it's too late."

"Who?"

But my little sister's eyes were already closed and she was snoring softly.

CHAPTER 18

Five days to go and our excitement at the upcoming big day almost obliterated the strange events of the night before. Corker had sent her letter to Santa sometime in November – and a follow-up one with our change of address – to make doubly sure there was no mistake in his rounds - the minute she knew we were moving to Tumble Cottage.

This morning she was talking Mum's ear off about the fairy costume she had asked for. Would Santa know her size? Would he remember the silver slippers? And, come to think of it, how about the wand? Had she remembered to include the wand in her letter to Lapland?

Jamie caught the bug and started rattling on at ten to the dozen about getting an X Box for Christmas. It seemed as if the twins' had genuinely forgotten their experience in the garden. Either that or I was going mad and had imagined the whole thing.

"Corker. What in heavens name have you been doing?" Dad's voice sounded loud in the kitchen as he held the offending items above his head for all to see. The colours of the sodden Barbie slippers had run so that the red trim now merged with the pink resulting in a spearmint goo effect.

"I found these under the settee in the little lounge," he said, looking at Mum as if she had put them there. "They're soaking wet. What's she been doing?"

"Wait a second and I'll go and get my crystal ball," said Mum slotting the plates slightly too firmly into the dishwasher. "How in heavens name am

I supposed to know. In case it has escaped your attention lately, she's your daughter too!"

As the argument developed, I saw my chance and slipped out unnoticed. Curiosity overcame my fear as I retraced our nocturnal expedition. The sky looked heavy with a threatening pink tinge, but for the moment it was dry. In broad daylight the evidence was there for all to see. The three sets of footprints were clearly visible as I made my way down the garden. Corker's smaller slipper tracks on the outward journey, followed by the bigger and more distinct impressions left by mine and Jamie's gumboots. Deeper marks at the edge of the fir trees, where Corker had stopped for the first time.

I turned and looked back at the house. Mum and Dad were still in the middle of their shouting match in the kitchen with Corker sitting as if butter wouldn't melt in her angelic mouth. Everything normal there then.

Moving on down the garden I found a major disturbance of the snow beside the holly bush – the site of my saving rugby tackle.

I stopped at the bush. Was this the point of no return? What would I find on the other side? A monster with glowing blue eyes? Worse – a dead baby lying frozen and blue in the snow.

I listened to the morning noises. The reassuring hum of traffic on the busy road half a mile away. The sudden, piercing call of a bird in a tree. The answering bark of a neighbouring dog. No unnatural sound, like a baby crying at the bottom of our garden.

Taking a final deep breath, I stepped beyond the holly bush into the third section.

Immediately my eyes were everywhere, sweeping the landscape for intruders. Ready for flight at any sign of danger. Nothing. Not a thing out of place. It was the perfect winter scene from a Christmas card. Just like the words in the famous carol, the snow lay deep and crisp and even. To the left, the bushes marking the entrance to the Reynard family house were heavy with undisturbed snow. To the right, the roof of the air raid shelter was covered in a thick layer that looked perfect and untouched. The ground in between was as white and smooth as the icing on a Wedding cake.

Breaking the ground with my own footprints somehow felt like sacrilege. But I had to investigate the whole area thoroughly in order to put my mind at ease.

Starting at the school fence on the foxhole side, I inched my way across the ground searching for the tiniest sign of trespass. There was none. Reaching the shelter, I hesitated once more, conscious that only the top storey of the house was visible from here. Then, cursing my silliness, I ducked inside.

My first sensation was of coldness. It was much colder inside the shelter than outside. I could see my breath streaming before me in plumes on the chill air. The place felt like a refrigerator, I thought as I stamped my feet on the dirty concrete floor. It also seemed smaller and gloomier now that all the tea chests had been removed and it was empty.

But I was wrong. It wasn't quite empty. There was an old cloth lying in the corner. At least that's what I thought it was until I picked it up. I had assumed it was a washing rag left by Mum when she was clearing the place out. But it felt dry and woollen and when I raised it to my face it smelled clean and fresh with a scent like roses. I must have stood like that for several minutes, hugging the wool to my face, breathing in its unexpected warmth and fragrance in the cold, gloomy shelter.

The long sigh was followed by a dull thud. I almost screamed into the wool and felt the hair on my arms prickle in the same way they had on the night when I first glimpsed Skankie. My head swivelled round the shelter. There was nothing here, but the noise had come from terribly near.

Then it happened again. The same long sigh accompanied by a heavier thud this time. It was right outside.

"Corks, Jamie. Is that you?" I stammered." Silence. "Jamie. If that's you I'll murder you," I screamed. No reply. I shifted from one foot to the other on the bare concrete floor. I wanted to wee. I needed desperately.

Deciding I would not wet myself in here, no matter what was waiting, I screamed and launched myself outside. At the same time the long sigh and thud happened again. I ducked and covered my head waiting for the whistle of the axe, or the sharp pain of a knife between my shoulder blades.

Nothing. Nothing but a wet bum from sitting in the snow with my hands over my eyes. Slowly I looked around to see absolutely no one there at all. Then I giggled with hysterical relief as I saw the source of the noise. The shelter's roof was now almost completely bare of snow and as I looked the last thick wedge fell with the same sigh and muffled thud I had heard inside the shelter.

I was so relieved that I almost forgot my woollen comforter. It was lying in the snow where I must have abandoned it in my fright. Now in the daylight I recognised what it really was and I felt the goosebumps rise on my arms again. It was a pink baby's shawl.

As I trudged back towards the house, past our footprints of the night before, I saw my old friend the Robyn Redbreast hopping around the snow searching for food. "You'll have to dig deep to find anything today," I said, and he cocked his head at me as if he understood every word. The thought dawned on me as I watched him fly to the branch of a bare tree.

The bottom of the garden was too perfect. When I examined it there were no tracks in the snow at all – not even the prints of birds.

First, the foxes had vanished and now the birds were giving the place a wide berth too. I had no idea what was causing the wildlife to abandon our garden beyond the trees. But I was determined to find out.

CHAPTER 19

It's tiny," said Corker, examining the shawl for the umpteenth time. "I wonder what RT stands for?"

"Radio Times," chirped Jamie attempting to pull the shawl away from Corker as she examined the small red letters sewn at the bottom.

"Jamie, that's enough. Stop winding her up or Mum will be up to investigate. We have to think about what we are going to do," I said quietening Corker's screech of protest.

We were in the twins' bedroom again with the Do Not Disturb sign on the door and Jamie's drawers once more barricading the entrance. But I was beginning to question my judgment in sharing my discovery with the twins. Jamie was larking about in his usual head-on-backwards fashion and Corker seemed only to be interested in purloining the shawl for her dolls.

"We have to get to the bottom of this," I said. "We have to find out what it is that is invading our garden every night. "Are you two going to help me, or do I have to do this on my own."

Jamie looked as if he was perfectly happy to let me go solo, but good old Corker came to my aid. "All for one, and one for all. Of course we'll help Alex. Won't we Jamie." Jamie merely grunted. But I took Corker's cue and launched my big idea.

"I'll tell you what we need," I said. "We need to establish some sort of early warning system. A kind of alarm to alert us whenever whatever it is that's coming into our garden arrives – if you see what I mean," I finished lamely.

By their blank looks the twins' clearly didn't have a clue what I was talking about, so I blurted out my idea.

"Mum's clothesline. We'll use Mum's clothesline and her chimes."

Jamie waggled a finger at his head and let his tongue loll. "Quick Corks, get the straightjacket, our sister's loony tunes."

I slapped his knee. "Listen you idiot. We string the clothesline in the back garden between the bushes and the shelter with the chimes on it. Then when whatever it is trips over it in the dark we'll know it's there and trap it."

"Oh yeah," scoffed Jamie, the clothesline isn't long enough. Anyway the chimes would ring whenever the wind blows, dummy."

I was about to fetch my smart-aleck brother a much harder smack around the head when he sat up straight.

"But I know what might work," Jamie said. "Although it will involve a special mission and we'll have to be very careful Mum and Dad don't find out what we're up to."

Later, under cover of darkness when Mum and Dad were safely tucked up in bed, we made our sortie down the garden.

Being his infuriating self, Jamie had refused point blank to disclose any further details of our adventure. And he insisted on leading the way, partially masking the beam of Mum's torch to keep the risk of us being spotted to a minimum. Of course, our parents were zeeing for England so there was absolutely no chance of them discovering us, and that night the garden was perfectly behaved without the slightest hint of strange noises or bizarre lights.

Reaching the shed, Jamie produced the key he had smuggled from the kitchen drawer and undid the padlock. The door opened with a creak, which sounded screechingly loud in the stillness, and we stood petrified, certain that at any moment the alarm would be raised at the house.

Eventually realising the coast was clear, Jamie trained the torch on the pitch black interior of the shed. The beam travelled slowly across the gleaming red tractor, over shelves stacked with splattered paint cans, jam jars stuffed with nails, flower pots, and a weedkiller tin bearing an ominous black skull and crossbones label, and came to rest on what looked like a wheel. Jamie grunted as he clambered over the tractor and reached up and brought the wheel down.

It turned out to be the only useful item the Pelejics left behind - a coil of wire. After a furious but silent dispute about who should do what, I finally agreed to hold the wheel at the bottom of the garden while Corker and Jamie paid out the line up to the house. They made it to the patio with about twenty feet of wire left.

Jamie reckoned it would just be about enough for his plan. Then he sent Corker back down to tell me to come up the garden making sure that the line stretched taught an inch above the snow from my end right up to the house.

"All right, what now?" I asked as we huddled together freezing on the patio. "Now you take one of your trainer's off," said Jamie with a superior smirk at my astonished expression.

"Okay, enough is enough Brain," I said. "Tell us this great scheme of yours right now, or Corker and I will lock you out here all night."

"Keep your hair on Alex. I was about to tell you. Anyway, I've given you the main part, so I don't know what you have to grumble about," he said grudgingly.

"I should think so to. The original idea was mine. Now get on with the explanation."

So Jamie did. And I have to admit it was a pretty neat plan. His idea was to take the wire up the wall to my bedroom and then through the window to the bedside table, where we would attach Mum's chimes. Jamie had already "borrowed" them from a box in the bottom of Mum's wardrobe. He needed my trainer, or rather one of the eyelets in my shoe, in order to thread the wire through so that it would go up the wall at right angles. As I hopped about the snow with one shoe on and one very cold stockinged foot, Corker and Jamie struggled to get the long set of ladders from the garage. With Corker and I holding them steady against the wall, Jamie climbed up to my bedroom with the wire and pushed the last three feet of line through the window.

"But what if Mum or Dad sees the wire, or finds my shoe for that matter?" I asked after the twins' had returned the ladder.

For the first time that night Jamie looked genuinely stumped. "Aha, caught you there clever clogs. Come on Corks, let's get the ladders again, we've got some dismantling to do."

"No wait," said Corker. "If they find it we can say it's a scientific experiment we're doing for a school project." Jamie nodded as if he had been about to make the very same suggestion. But I was forced to agree with Corker. Her answer sounded a pretty good solution to any nosey questions from interfering parents. So the last thing I did before going to bed was to attach Mum's chimes to the wire on my bedroom night table.

Chapter 20

It wasn't our science experiment, but the sound of a plane that wakened me that night. Rolling over to check the digital clock, I rubbed my eyes in disbelief. The luminous red numbers showed 3.30. Surely that couldn't be right. There had to be some law against planes flying over houses at such ungodly hours of the morning. I was certain I had heard Dad talking about what he called "aviation legislation" before we bought Tumble Cottage.

Well, no matter what the aviation legislation said, there was a thumping great aeroplane above us right now making a colossal noise. In fact it sounded as though it was directly over our house. The heavy drone of the engine sounded very different to the jets that passed overhead during the day. There was something else. This plane sounded slower and – judging from the huge din – it was flying much lower in the sky than usual.

As I covered my ears the vibrations started to shake the furniture in my room.

I leapt from my bed and ran out on to the landing, where I nearly collided with the twins'. "What's happening Alex? Is it an earthquake?" asked Jamie. Despite my own fright, I noticed with a surge of affection that my little brother was holding his little sister's hand. "My bed was shaking. I'm scared," whimpered Corker.

"Don't worry. It's all right," I said cuddling them both. "They don't get earthquakes in Surrey. It's just a noisy plane."

At that moment I realised two things. Mum and Dad were not preparing to evacuate the house. Secondly, the hall was completely silent. "Wait there," I said, and tip-toeing along to my parents bedroom, I cracked open the door a couple of inches. Peering into the gloom, I managed to see – and hear – enough to know that they had somehow slept through the entire episode. There was the vague outline of Mum on her side with a pillow crammed over her head. Dad was lying flat out beside her snoring loud enough to open and shut windows with his feet sticking out the end of the duvet.

Carefully closing their door, I returned to the twins'. "I don't know how they didn't hear it, but they're both asleep," I said. "Anyway the plane's gone now. Quick, let's get back to bed before they do waken up."

Dog tired, I opened my bedroom door again - only to be assailed by the thunderous drone of engines and the continuing disintegration of the room. I watched with terrified fascination as my wardrobe rocked dangerously and all my dolls fell off the windowsill. The china clown my grandmother had given me seemed to bounce across the carpet in slow motion. It came to rest at my feet and as I gazed at the black glass eyes and the painted smile, a tiny crack appeared in its porcelain neck and its head rolled off.

Stifling a scream, I slammed the door shut and stood shivering in the silent hall as a wave of dizziness and nausea swept over me. I would almost certainly have been sick had the twins' not re-joined me. One look at their faces told me the same story. "Not gone?" I whispered. "Not gone," they agreed, quaking as our bedrooms quaked.

The shout boomed through the night like a ship's fog-horn sending us into another terrified huddle.

"Hey. Hey younguns. What do you think you are doing? Don't you know the regulations? Get those lights out and be smart about it."

The voice was deep and commanding; one that demanded immediate obedience. Staring through the hall window, we saw its owner.

He was standing at the foot of the front lawn in approximately the same place as Skankie had been when I glimpsed him for the first time. But whereas Skankie was frail and shuffling, this man was a giant. The street lighting made it difficult to see him properly. But Jamie, an expert in all things military, confirmed what my eyes registered, but my brain refused to accept.

"It's a soldier – an old war soldier," breathed Jamie.

The man wore a helmet, shaped like the ones I had seen in our school history books. He was so big it looked like a pea on his head. It was impossible to tell the colour of his uniform in the darkness, but a sixth sense told me it was khaki. The crossbands straining across his great chest, the belt boots and puttees, unmistakably marked him out as a soldier from the Second World War. A haversack was slung across one massive shoulder. A cord hung around his bull neck attached to a glint of silver, which I made out to be a whistle. At his waist I saw the menacing outline of a pistol butt in a leather holster. He was carrying a long wooden pole with a hook on the end.

"I won't say it a second time you pups," he said in a voice that seemed to come from his boots. "Blackout conditions is the law in air raids. I'm the Warden that enforces the law. Lights out now children and get to bed before the Warden has to come and enforce the law."

For a split second his eyes seemed to be on fire as he glared up at us fingering the handle of his gun. It was enough. Jamie jumped like a scalded cat in his speed to switch off the hall light. "That's good. Sleep tight, don't let the bed bugs bite," he growled.

Deep, piratical laughter rumbled in our ears as he raised the pole to the street lamp. Then with a flick of his mighty wrist, like a magician waving a wand, he snuffed out the light and his giant frame was enveloped by the darkness.

It was only when I was back in bed, thankfully in a room that was once more blissfully quiet, that I realised something else that was as impossible as the sight of a giant Second World War soldier outside our house in the dead of night.

The street lamp he had put out was entirely *different* from our normal one. Our normal one was tall. It required men on lorries with special cranes to get up high enough to fix the lamp when it needed to be repaired. I had seen them doing it to the same kind of lights in our old street in Yorkshire. A man with a pole, even a giant, could never have reached it.

It was also electric with a bright orange light. The lamp the Warden had extinguished was much smaller with a flickering yellow light and a post that looked more like iron than concrete. It hadn't looked modern. It had looked "old fashioned."

Chapter 21

The hospital was still and peaceful. The chaotic bustle of day had given way to the quiet watchfulness of night. The phones were mostly silent on the big reception desk – allowing the clerk to watch a small portable TV in the inner office. And the long, green corridors were empty – except for the solitary figure of a cleaning lady shining the faded linoleum with her electric mop.

Behind the double doors of the Intensive Care Unit things were quieter still. The small corridor was bathed in a calming green glow reminiscent of the illumination on the dashboard of a motorcar, or the instrument panel of an aeroplane. The same muted lighting bathed the half dozen patients who lay motionless in beds behind the long glass windows. Nothing stirred – apart from the constant tick of the large ward clock and the occasional whisper of life-sustaining fluids running through the battery of tubes at each bedside.

The rosy-cheeked Ward Sister had just completed her rounds and was taking a well earned break as she sat in her small office with her feet up, eating a chocolate bar and reading a copy of Cheerio magazine.

She had just reached a particularly interesting series of exclusive pictures showing the wedding of a pop star to a supermodel when a red light on the wall above her head started to blink and beep.

The Ward Sister's shoes squeaked rapidly across the highly polished floor as she ran to the source of the alarm.

The green lines on the screen monitor at the patient's bedside had suddenly changed from average-size hills to jagged mountains. And the peaks were moving closer together and coming faster and faster. For the first time since being admitted to hospital Skankie's eyes were open – wide open. It was the terror in the old man's eyes that shocked the Ward Sister as he repeated the same four words over and over again – "hands in the fire."

CHAPTER 22

The lamp post at the foot of our front lawn was the same one we had seen every day since coming to live at Tumble Cottage. No magical force had spirited it away during the night. A crew of council workers had not been working overtime to uproot the modern light and substitute and old fashioned one in its place. Just to make sure, we all tapped it with our gloved fists and Corker kicked it with her Pocahontas gum boots for good measure. Nope. Same old solid- as- a -rock concrete lamp post.

But Corker wasn't finished there. Ignoring the fact that it was the coldest morning of the winter so far – and Jamie and I were desperate to get back inside for breakfast – she decided she was in a Sherlock mood.

"Clues Alex," she said, pursing her lips and jutting her chin out with an elfin glint in her hazel eyes. "Remember Skankie's milk bottles. They were clues that somebody lived in the house."

"Oh be quiet Corker. This is stupid. It's the same stupid lamp post. It must have been a hall … a hallunication you had Alex. I'm starving. It's sausages. I can smell them. Come on. Let's go," said Jamie.

"Hallucination, the word's hallucination," I said. "Come on, it won't hurt to spend five minutes looking for clues will it?"

"What kind of clues," Jamie grunted.

"Footprints," cried Corker with the kind of enthusiasm reserved for great scientific discoveries. "The giant's footprints."

"Duh. Oh yeah, I forgot, the giant's footprints. That was probably another hall… hallucination," Jamie said scoffing at his little sister's silliness. Even so, I caught him throw a furtive glance at the ground surrounding the lamp post.

While Jamie grumbled and smacked a stick against the lamp post, Corker and I patrolled the pavement searching for very large boot prints in the snow. There were none. It was as if we truly had imagined seeing the giant soldier. But how could all of us have imagined the same thing? That was impossible too, just as impossible as the soldier disappearing into thin air.

I didn't know what to think any more. All I knew for sure was that my head hurt from the cold and my stomach was grumbling for food. "Come on Corker, Jamie's right and I'm starving, let's go and get breakfast."

Jamie and I were half way back to the front door when we heard Corker's triumphant shriek. "Clues Jamie. Clues!" she yelled running towards us with one arm punching the sky.

I looked in bewilderment at the object she had placed in my hand. "This doesn't mean anything Corks," I said staring at the small brass ring.

"No. That's where you're wrong," said Jamie, taking the ring and turning it over in his fingers. "I know what this is from and where to find it. Come on, follow me."

Jamie raced back to the house and pelted upstairs, pausing only to post Corker on sentry duty in the hall with instructions to sing loudly should Mum or Dad emerge from the kitchen.

On the landing he grabbed the pole for opening the loft, unhooked the trapdoor, pulled down the ladder and was scrambling up through the hatch before I could catch my breath to ask him what on earth he was doing.

His orders sailed down from the darkness. "Hold the ladders steady for me Alex, I'll be down in a minute."

"Yes sir!" I said sarcastically. Normally I would have shot my little brother down in flames for having the cheek to tell me what to do. There was a distinct pecking order among the three of us and I was definitely number one. But Jamie was usually such a couch potato that Mum nick-named him TV Tim. I had rarely seen him so excited about anything, so I was surprised and secretly pleased about the effect this mysterious mission was having on him.

For several minutes all I could hear from the loft were the sounds of a mad stampede – crashing, rustling noises and the occasional ominous thud of what sounded like something heavy being tossed aside.

"Jamie, you better not make a mess up there or Dad will have a fit," I warned, knowing only too well my brother's carelessness with other people's belongings.

Suddenly the thumping stopped and Jamie's face appeared in the hatchway grinning from ear to ear. "Got it!" he exclaimed, before scampering back down the ladder and springing from the second last rung like a circus acrobat.

His face was smudged with dirt and there was a large bulge beneath his fleece. "What have you got there?" I said trying to poke his stomach.

"Wait a minute," he said, squirming away. "Corker," he whispered over the balcony. "You can come upstairs now."

Jamie obviously wanted to bask in his moment of glory before the widest possible audience. I felt like bashing him with the loft pole as he stood with his nose in the air.

When Corker arrived he addressed us like a distinguished professor lecturing a class of particularly dim students.

"Dad had one when he was at primary. He kept his schoolbooks in it. He showed it to us all once, but you two obviously don't remember," he said in an extremely irritating know-all voice.

"Oh get on with it, or I'll hit you," I said reaching for the loft pole.

"There's no need to be like that Alex," he said huffily. Then with an extravagant flourish, he lifted his fleece and removed the mystery object in a cloud of dust.

"It's a haversack," spluttered Corker as we all coughed and sneezed on the landing.

"Exactly!" said Jamie, and the brass ring suddenly appeared in his other hand. He held it alongside Dad's haversack.

"The ring we found is from the strap of a haversack – an old army haversack like Dad's. But there are no rings missing from Dad's haversack see."

We looked and saw that the two brass rings attaching either end of the strap to the bag were still there on Dad's old school bag.

"There can only be one explanation," I murmured. "We didn't imagine it. He really was here. The brass ring we found in the snow is from the giant's haversack."

PART 3

The Warden

CHAPTER 23

The day John Crow was born the world stopped. The still, silent entrance of Agnes Crow's son to life in a dingy delivery room in the Royal London Hospital, Whitechapel, on February 4, 1901, was mirrored by a deathly hush on the snow-covered streets of the metropolis.

The great teaching hospital, in common with every other public building in the city, was swathed in imperial purple and white funeral drapes. Union Jacks throughout the capital fluttered at half- mast and church bells tolled a last mournful farewell to an aged monarch who had ruled an empire embracing a quarter of the globe.

As the horses of the Royal Artillery shook their noble heads, snorting nervous plumes of steam into the chill morning air, and the blue-jacketed sailors strained on the drag ropes of Queen Victoria's coffin, the midwives fought to release John Crow from the body of his mother.

It had been a mighty struggle. All night and half the morning Agnes had fought to deliver her son and her strength was waning.

"Just one more push Agnes. I can see the shoulders. You're almost there darlin,'" urged the small Irish nurse, and with a final superhuman effort, the mother pushed her newborn into the world.

"Mother of mercy. He's blue. He's not breathing. The cord was round his neck. It's strangled him!" screamed the nurse.

"Control yourself woman," commanded the Matron as she shoved the nurse out of the way and snatched the baby up in her arms.

Rushing behind a screen, the Matron placed the lifeless baby on a scarred wooden table, eased a tube between his blue lips, and began to blow.

"What's happening? What have you done with my baby?" The exhausted, desperate wail of the mother drove the Matron on to greater efforts.

The mother had battled for 15 hours to bring her child into the world. What kind of world it would be for a waif brought up in the abject poverty of the East End without a father and a streetwalker for a mother, the Matron could barely imagine. But she had rarely seen a woman endure so much pain without a single curse, or word of complaint. Such sacrifice should have its reward, the Matron thought as she blew into the tube and massaged the tiny chest.

She looked up at the clock on the drab brown walls. Three minutes. She had been giving the baby the kiss of life for three minutes now without the faintest movement. The sands of time were running out for him.

The Matron made her decision as she watched the minutes' hand continue its relentless journey inside the yellowing glass. It was at the Roman numeral III. When it had reached the beginning of its next minute cycle at XII she would stop. Forty-five seconds in which to kindle a spark of life, or consign the baby to the grave.

She renewed her efforts – puffing draughts of air down the tube and massaging the lifeless heart between her thumb and forefinger. At VI, the tube appeared to shiver, like a blade of grass stroked by the gentlest breeze.

The Matron frowned in concentration. Perhaps she had been trying too hard and moved the tube herself without realising it. She stopped and counted off two vital seconds.

At VII, the tube wobbled again – and this time she knew the pressure was coming upwards from the tiny blue lips. Was it a trick of the gaslight, or was there a tinge of colour creeping over his frozen mouth? She started blowing again and at VIV the baby's chest heaved and he coughed.

Picking him up by the feet, the Matron slapped his bottom twice and John Crow emitted the first sound of his brutal life, mewling like a kitten as, in an instant, he turned from ice-blue to outraged crimson.

"Eleven pounds, nine ounces. Heavens above, that's not a baby, it's a cannon ball, Agnes," announced the Matron plucking the baby from the weighing scales. Wrapping him in a course blanket, she whisked the screen aside like a magician performing a particularly clever conjuring trick.

"Well, I tell you he gave us a scare, but he's here now. Here's your son," she said moving towards the head of the bed. "Mrs Crow, waken up and see your son. Poor woman, she's done in. Molly, give her a nudge, she'll want to see him – and judging from his shrieks, she'll need to feed the poor mite before she gets any rest," laughed the Matron.

Beaming, the Irish nurse patted the mother. "Come on Agnes. Look who's here to see you." Agnes Crow slumped sideways on her pillow and her eyes stared sightlessly at the ceiling.

The Matron picked up her wrist, felt for a pulse, and – with a deep sigh - replaced the hand gently back on the bed.

"In the end it was just too much for you dear. There wasn't much for you in this life, let's hope the next one's better. God bless you and keep you Agnes Crow," said the Matron closing the mother's eyes.

"Take the sheets down to the laundry Molly, they'll need boiling. Tell the mortuary attendants we want them up here straight away. Oh, and we'll need to organise some milk for this greedy little chap."

Crossing herself, the Irish nurse scurried from the room with the blood-soaked sheets.

The Matron looked down at the baby now screaming himself purple in her arms. She could still see the mark round his neck where his mother's cord had tightened like a hangman's noose, threatening to choke the life from him.

She wasn't superstitious like Molly, but it occurred to her that nature had played the cruellest of tricks on this bitter winter morning. First, the boy had almost been strangled by his mother's umbilical cord. Then, in the act of being born, the son had killed his mother. It was as if the two people who needed each other most in the world had attempted to murder each other. But the child had survived. He had been the stronger of the two and shown his incredible will to live. What omen did his extraordinary birth portend for the boy's future?

Her thoughts were shattered by the boom of cannon. "They're saluting the dead queen, John Crow," she whispered. The infant's eyes snapped open and he became perfectly quiet, as though entranced by the gunfire.

Chapter 24

The eagle had been caught in mid-flight. Above the scimitar beak its piercing eyes were focused on an unseen prey; its needle sharp talons spread wide in preparation for a kill that would forever escape its grasp.

When John Crow had first arrived at the house his uncle had picked him up and held him close enough to the bird for the boy to see the dried blood encrusted on its talons. Crow had screamed and scampered behind the mouse-infested settee as fast as his stubby legs would carry him. But his uncle had dragged him back and held him up to the bird until his screams died away to exhausted croaks.

"There's a lesson in this boy," he said as the child thrashed uselessly to escape. "The mighty eagle is king of all he surveys. You see them talons," he said, forcing the boy's face against the jagged claws. "Them talons has ripped apart a thousand lesser creatures. Dipped 'emselves in the guts of rats, torn the innards out of rabbits, aye, maybe even taken human blood."

He whispered conspiratorially in the boy's ear. "Maybe, when an unsuspecting mother's back was turned, maybe even scooped up the odd baby or two from its pram for a midnight feast on some cliff ledge." The man's mad cackle echoed through the gloomy house. "Yet he's 'ere. Mr High-an'-Mighty Bleedin' Eagle, sitting stuffed on the mantel in your uncle's parlour.

"What does that tell you John Crow? How does that improve your educatin'?" he shouted as the boy shook with fear. "I'll tell you, you snivelling brat. It tells you that nature is red in tooth and claw and folk is the same. Folk'll cheat and lie and rob you blind boy. Them's the rules they live by, so we have to live by 'em better. Be tougher, stronger, more ruthless like Mr Eagle here. Otherwise we gets gutted like all them rats and rabbits," he said drawing a rough, calloused hand across the boy's stomach. "If you can't learn that, you'll be useless to me and I'll dump you back in that orphanage faster'n I found you."

Almost ten years had passed since that first harsh lesson. In that time the boy had learned many more hard facts of life. The beatings were always accompanied by his uncle's homespun sayings such as "where there's a will there's a way", "spare the rod and ruin the child", and his favourite – "idle hands make mischief."

Not that Crow had time to be idle. His Uncle Bird, for that was his nick-name in the trade, was a scrap metal merchant. He owned a junkyard in the East End with a great wrought iron sign above the entrance proclaiming 'Bird's Paraphernalia'. He worked the boy from dawn till dark scavenging for bric-a-brac around the neighbourhood in a cart pulled by an old piebald named One Eye. The unfortunate horse had lost the other one when Uncle Bird had taken a whip to it in a drunken rage.

Crow had lost count of the times he had been locked up in a shed in the back of the yard on a diet of mouldy bread and watery cabbage soup when Uncle Bird thought the boy was shirking. But the whip had never been used on him for the simple reason that he was too valuable to his uncle.

Only 13 and a half and an inch short of six foot, Crow was a wonderful asset to the scrap metal business. Despite the poor rations, over the years the boy's strength had grown in step with his height and now Crow could lift almost as much as the man.

The boy was about to prove his worth as fate took a dramatic hand in his destiny. Far away in a foreign country called Bosnia an important man called Archduke Franz Ferdinand was assassinated by members of a secret terror-ist organisation known as the Black Hand. His murder led to the start of the First World War and the outbreak of fighting between Britain and Germany.

The Great War meant death and destruction for millions of soldiers on both sides. For a ruthless few, however, it spelled a wonderful business opportunity. The British army desperately needed as many guns and tanks as it could muster for the terrible battles ahead and Uncle Bird was in a state of high excitement at the prospect.

"This war will make me a rich man, mark my words boy," he said as they sat one night eating their meagre supper in the gloomy parlour.

"I don't understand uncle," said Crow as he wolfed into a bread and dripping sandwich. "What does the war have to do with us?"

"Think Crow," Bird snarled, grabbing the boy's hair and shaking his head so hard that his teeth rattled and bits of his supper flew from his mouth. "Use whatever useless rusty brain that trollop of a mother gave you for a change, instead of them stupid big muscles. What do we do?" He asked the question slowly spelling out each word.

"Collect junk uncle?"

Yes, yes, but what kind of junk?"

"Well, all kinds – tables, chairs, that old stove the other day from the old woman in Solomon Street. Remember how I got it out the back of her house and on to the cart while you…."

Uncle Bird pushed the boy's head away in disgust. "Steel boy. And metal. Metal and steel is the answer. Our brave lads on the front line is goin' to need hundreds of thousands of rifles and bullets and bayonets to kill them Jerries and that's where Bird's Paraphernalia comes in." He jabbed a proud finger at his own chest. "As scrap and metal merchants it'll be our patriotic duty to King an' country to collect as much metal as possible for our glorious troops."

At this point Bird cackled so hard that he was in danger of choking on his own supper. "So we'll have to work double hard at borrowing every pot and pan, knife and fork, stove and lamp we can from all our lovely neighbours. Then we'll flog 'em to the government armaments factories for a whackin' great profit," he yelled, and tears of laughter rolled down his filthy unshaven cheeks as he crashed his fists on top of the table. "This war's a bloody godsend boy. Bird's Paraphernalia is goin' up in the world. I'm goin' to be filthy rich."

CHAPTER 25

In the months that followed Uncle Bird was as good as his word. As the slaughter in the trenches of France grew ever more terrible, he and Crow worked night and day travelling the local streets collecting scrap metal until their cart was crammed so full that One Eye could barely pull the weight back to the yard.

Then one day One Eye's legs buckled, the faithful old horse fell to the ground and no amount of Uncle Bird's whipping or swearing could stir him. "Bloody thing's gone and died on me. Fit for nothing now but the knacker's yard," Bird cursed as he aimed a final kick at One Eye's head before stamping off up the street.

That night – under cover of a thick, swirling fog – fire and terror rained down on London.

The Zeppelin was Germany's secret weapon at the beginning of the Great War. Huge whale-shaped airships, Zeppelins were filled with a gas called hydrogen, enabling them to travel great distances at high altitude. Bristling with machine-guns and loaded with bombs, fleets of Zeppelins carried out regular night raids on London causing widespread panic and destruction.

Despite his size, Crow found himself quaking with fear as he hid in the shed, where he had been so regularly imprisoned, and listened to the Zeppelin attack. He didn't know what was worse – waiting for the explosions, or the explosions themselves. For what felt like eons of time there was complete silence as Crow stared at the ceiling, almost willing himself to see through the roof slates into the sky above.

Then he would hear the sound of the monster coming. The slow, rhythm of its breathing sounding like the mighty swish of a dragon's tail as the gas whooshed into the giant billowing canvas lungs and the Zeppelin sailed closer. Once, one seemed to hover directly overhead and – praying for the first time in his life – Crow strained to hear the whistle of the bomb that would signal his destruction. But the prehistoric bellows began once more and the monster sailed on.

Half an hour later the boy heard his uncle entering the yard accompanied by the clatter of hooves. Peeping through a slit in the shed door he saw the silhouette of Bird swaying as he struggled to hold the reigns of a horse, while ransacking his trouser pockets at the same time. A small torrent of coins fell to the ground, followed by the house keys and Bird swore as he bent – and then fell – in his efforts to pick them up. The horse looked disinterestedly at the drunken man as he grovelled around on the cobblestones for his possessions.

"Crow. Where are you, you good-for-nothin' boy? I bought another horse. This un's got two eyes," he giggled. "Cost me an arm and a leg from this swindler at the Dog and Duck. Crow! Get out here before I tan your hide."

This was a bad turn of events. Uncle Bird was nasty enough sober, but when he had been drinking an even nastier side to his character revealed itself. Crow sighed deeply as he opened the shed door and stepped into the yard.

"Ah, there you are you lazy brat. Come on, we've work to do."

"What work uncle?"

"The cart, you idiot. We've got to get the cart back before our good-for-nuthin' neighbours steal the wheels and everything else."

"Nobody's goin' to steal anythin' uncle. Nobody's goin' anywhere. We're in the middle of an air raid."

As if to prove Crow's point, a great explosion went off nearby shaking the ground and, for a brief second, a flash of orange punctured the fog.

The horse whinnied in fright and reared as its back legs skidded on the cobblestones. "We've got to get inside uncle," shouted Crow attempting to take the man's arm and guide him to the front door.

With a furious shake, Bird pushed the boy's hand away and reached for the whip in his jacket. "Spare the rod, spoil the child. I've been far too soft with you boy. Bein' related I suppose clouded my judgment. But no more. It stops here, tonight. You've had this comin' for a long time." With that, Bird uncurled the whip and lurched towards Crow.

He was three feet away when – with a great boom - the white mist was burned away and for a blinding moment night turned to day. The swirling canopy of the airship collapsed in a sea of blue flames and fell, like dead skin over the roof, while the vessel's hull crashed through the house shearing the sign, Bird's Paraphernalia, into two precise pieces between the s and the P.

One second the horse was in the yard rearing in wild panic, the next it was simply blown apart in a shower of ink-black blood and the cobblestones shone wet with boiling intestines, a severed hoof and the stump of a brown singed tail.

Uncle Bird's whip had reached the top of its wicked backswing when a piece of flying shrapnel sliced his head neatly from his shoulders. Thanks to his nose and ears, the head bounced unevenly across the yard before coming to rest – face up and mouth open as if in the process of uttering another curse - by the springs of an old iron bedspread.

John Crow checked his own head and the rest of his body. Apart from feeling very hot and slightly singed, he didn't find so much as a scratch. As he ran from the yard, he didn't look back once, even when – with a final creaking groan – the walls collapsed and his uncle's scrap metal merchant's business was flattened to the ground.

CHAPTER 26

John Crow didn't go far for the simple reason that there was nowhere to go. The orphanage Uncle Bird had plucked him from held nothing but bad memories and – even if he had wanted to return – he doubted whether they would have taken him back. Orphanages were for children and he was so large he now looked more like an adult than a child – even if he was still small and terrified on the inside.

So he waited for the soldiers and the fire brigade to clear up after the Zeppelin raid, and then he went back to the place he knew best.

Bird's Paraphernalia had been reduced to rubble and was little more than a building site, but the shed had miraculously escaped unscathed and Crow made that his home.

No one noticed or cared. In the chaos of war the boy was only one among thousands of other children throughout London who had lost parents, or guardians and were now alone in the world and forced to look after themselves.

He was better off than most. At least he had a roof over his head. Many children in the East End were homeless. They slept in draughty alleys, or under railway bridges at night and wandered the streets begging for scraps of food during the day.

Crow had another advantage. Not only was he physically much bigger than his fellow urchins, he was street smart. In Uncle Bird he had experienced the toughest training from the best teacher in the craft of survival. In the years that lay ahead he would use every one of those black arts to swindle and cheat the weak and profit from the misfortune of others.

Of course he never became rich. John Crow possessed a rat-like cunning, but he didn't have the intelligence to lift himself above the role of simply being a big bully.

And he was big. Enormously big. By the age of 16 he had grown to 6ft 3ins – and by 18 (the age when most people stop growing) he was 6ft 5ins – and still growing. He finally stopped at 20 when, in his socks, he stood at the truly gigantic height of 6ft 7ins.

For almost the next 20 years Crow scraped a living as a Jack-of-all-trades – master of none. Like his Uncle Bird, he grew meaner as he grew older and delighted in being nasty for its own sake. But, unlike Bird, he also grew lazier, and like most lazy people, he didn't have the energy to pull himself up by his size 18 boot-laces and do something about his lack of success. He spent his time wasting his time by waiting for something extraordinary to happen. Something that would change his life forever. Then, in 1939, at the age of 39, it did.

CHAPTER 27

It was a sunny Sunday morning in September and Crow had just finished pretending to repair a pensioner's roof for ten shillings – a complete swindle as he had only made a noise shifting a couple of tiles around and hadn't fixed them properly at all – when a chillingly familiar noise gave him such a fright he almost fell off his ladders.

Leaping down like a scalded cat, Crow scrunched into as small a ball as his huge body would allow and clapped his hands over his ears in a frantic attempt to drown out the terrifying wail of the air raid sirens. "Please no God, not the Zeppelins again, please no," he chanted over and over again with his eyes squeezed tight shut.

But, instead of the dread whistle of a bomb, he heard the jolly tring of a bicycle bell. "Hey mate. It's all right, you can get up." Crow opened his eyes to see the stern face of a policeman. He was wearing a large notice board on his uniform, which said "Take Cover" in large black letters. "It's a false alarm. No bombs this time, but we're at war with Germany. It's official. The Prime Minister just announced it on the radio," added the officer as he pedalled on spreading the news down the street.

The giant heaved a giant sigh of relief and climbed shakily to his feet. He would get back to the shed as fast as he could and stay there until this horrible war was over.

But, as he carted his ladders along Solomon Street, other greedy thoughts crowded out the fearful ones.

What would Uncle Bird have done in this situation? Well, he knew the answer to that question. Uncle Bird had seen the First World War as a great opportunity and had been on the way to becoming very rich – before he lost his head.

Hmm. Crow's massive brow knitted together in a frown of immense concentration. Then he giggled. Uncle Bird had lost his head. He'd made a joke! But Crow wouldn't be so careless. He would use his head and make lots of money from the misfortune of others in this war in the same way that Uncle Bird had planned to do in the last one.

The first thing that struck Crow was the realisation that he would be too old to fight. He was almost 40. The government would take all the young men and put them in the army and leave him at home.

That suited Crow very well for two reasons. First, he was as big a coward as he was a bully and second, he could take advantage of the confusion and panic of war for his own selfish ends.

Now all he had to do was sit in his shed and watch and wait for his opportunity.

That chance came a few months later when the government asked for volunteers for what they called the Home Guard – a special army of older men formed to defend the country against enemy invasion.

Crow couldn't think of anything more frightening than being shot at by Germans, but the Home Guard had other duties besides training to fight. And Crow sensed a wonderful opportunity in those other duties. Members of the Home Guard also acted as air raid wardens.

What appealed to Crow was the fact that wardens had power over their fellow citizens. It was their job to make certain that everyone obeyed blackout regulations by putting out all the lights in their houses and pulling their specially made dark curtains tight shut during any attack by German planes. If anyone disobeyed those rules the warden had the right to enter and search the house.

Following an air raid it was also the duty of the wardens' to recover casualties and sound the "all-clear" with the whistles they wore around their necks. Crow was among the first to volunteer to become a warden.

His new job didn't exactly get off to the start he had hoped for. He found himself standing in a cold and draughty school gym on a rain-sodden night listening to the Chief Warden lecturing him about the importance of gas masks.

"Gas masks," said the Chief Warden, "is the first line of defence for the civilian against air attacks. Who knows what sort of poison Jerry might drop on top of us. So we have to be prepared. Every civilian must take their gas mask everywhere with them and be able to put it on within 10 seconds. That's the maximum time limit Crow. Anyone failing to get their mask on within that period risks being overcome by lethal fumes and after that ... well the end doesn't bear thinking about. But it would be very nasty, I can tell you." As if to emphasise the seriousness of his point the Chief Warden, who had a very large angry-looking red nose, gave it a loud honk on a piece of newspaper. Crow couldn't help wondering how the man managed to get his own gas mask over his huge conk within the 10-second time limit.

"Any questions Crow?" Crow shook his head. "Good. Taking information in first time. That's what I like to see my lad. You'll go far in the Home Guard. All you have to do now is fit the gas masks for our customers. They'll be here in about half an hour. Meantime, I'm off for a cuppa. Just give me a shout if you want any help."

"How many customers Chief?"

"'Bout three... four hundred. 'Pends how many streets we're doing tonight. Shouldn't take you any more than three hours. Then again, I've seen me still 'ere gone midnight. 'Pends on how many kids turn up. They can be a right pain in the backside, bawlin' and screamin' when your just tryin' to do somethin' that could save their lives. You think their parents would tell 'em it's for their own good." The Chief gave a parting wave as his back disappeared through the gymn's double doors and Crow's heart sank.

What a fool he had been volunteering for this. It was no better than being an unpaid baby-sitter for any Tom, Dick or Harry that cared to wander in off the street. To think he'd imagined there could be anything in it for him.

And now, to top it all, he could feel a cold coming on. Maybe he'd caught it from Big Chief Red Nose he thought miserably. His nose was imitating a melting icicle and his feet were frozen blocks at the end of his legs.

He looked around the dismal hall. There wasn't so much as a paraffin heater to ease the biting chill. Just the usual smelly gym equipment – oh, and stacks of cardboard coffins lined up against the wallbars. They were purely a precautionary measure, the Chief Warden had said. If the air raids caused thousands of civilian deaths the bodies would be put in these cardboard coffins and disposed of in mass graves of quicklime. Exactly the sort of cheerful image he needed on a miserable night like this, Crow thought as he sniffed hugely and gulped down the contents. His stomach heaved in protest and he realised that even he couldn't spend the night swallowing snot.

He emptied the contents of his haversack searching for something to blow his nose with. A torch, a rope, a first aid kit and a sewing kit fell out. Everything but a handkerchief.

Even though the gym was deserted he still checked before drawing the back of his sleeve across his nose. The action left a stream of green snot, glistening like a snail trail, across the khaki uniform. He wiped it on the underside of the long trestle table heaped with gas masks.

He was shovelling the contents back into the haversack when the needle from the sewing kit pricked him. He cursed and sucked the bleeding finger. That was the last straw. Joining the Home Guard was supposed to give him opportunities to line his own pockets. Not freeze to death in a smelly school gym waiting to fit gas masks to a bunch of snotty kids and their ungrateful parents. Somebody was going to pay for this.

The idea came to him as he continued sucking on his finger. He looked at the clock at the end of the hall. What had the Chief said? Half an hour before they turned up?

He picked up the needle and the first gas mask. He pushed the point through the rubber and studied the result – a tiny pin-prick virtually invisible to the naked eye. How much poisoned gas could get through that minute hole, he wondered. Enough to kill a person? There was no way he could know the answer to that question. No more than there was any way he could know how many gas masks he could prick in half an hour – unless he tried.

By the time the first horrible child burst through the double doors – followed by what looked like an endless line of whining children and adults – Crow had punctured 350 masks. He forced a smile and tried a line that he'd heard once at a fairground when he was a child. "Roll up, roll up." Then he added his own verses. "Get your gas masks here. No fee, fitted free." Free, but fatal, he hoped, and began to snigger so hard that everyone stared at him as though he was mad, which, of course, he was.

CHAPTER 28

Things started to look up for Crow when he was assigned to blackout duties. During the war all the lights in cities were switched off at night in case of enemy bombing raids – including the street lighting – and London became a dark and dangerous place.

The number of road accidents doubled, drivers often found themselves on the wrong side of the road, or spent hours going round in circles. Even pedestrians had problems finding their way home in the pitch black conditions.

But such extreme precautions were necessary because the dangers in the skies above London were very real.

The Great Blitz of London began on September 7 – only four days after Britain officially declared war on Germany. A mighty armada of 1,000 German planes, covering 800 square miles of sky, dropped their bombs on the capital. In that first momentous raid 430 civilians died and 1,600 were injured. Over the next 18 months two and a quarter million people were made homeless – 1 in 6 of them were Londoners.

Those who had no homes left to return to, or who were caught in London during the air raids, took cover in a series of refuges hastily constructed to meet the emergency. Trenches were dug in the parks, the basements of houses were reinforced, concrete and corrugated iron sheds called Anderson Shelters were dug in back gardens, and brick shelters were built on street pavements throughout the city.

Thousands of Londoners sheltered every night in the Underground stations. Whole families brought food and bedding down to the train platforms and people even slept on the wooden escalators. To keep their spirits up the crowds sang pop tunes of the time together and played games while the bombs fell.

The worst of the bombing hit the East End, so the blackout regulations had to be obeyed and people who left lights on in their houses, or didn't close the curtains properly, faced court appearances and heavy fines.

Wardens were responsible for enforcing the blackout regulations - and Crow was determined to enforce them to the letter of the law. He had never been happier than when patrolling the near deserted streets under cover of darkness.

Then one night, when a soup-thick fog rolled in off the Thames enveloping London in a white blanket – the sirens sounded their alarm.

A red, orange and yellow rainbow of thunderous flashes splintered the fog and Crow quickened his pace in the search for shelter. But a glimmer of light showing through a slit in a curtain made him pause as greed outweighed his fear.

He knew this house. It belonged to an old woman who lived on her own. "Lights. Get those lights out," he yelled, battering on the door with fists as big as dinner plates.

The minutes passed. The massive din of the exploding bombs frayed his nerves as they seemed to creep ever closer. CRUMP! CRASH! KABOOM! Hopping from foot to foot in his anxiety, he opened the letter-box and shouted into the hallway.

"It's the Warden. Open up in there. We're in the middle of an air raid. You're showing lights."

Eventually, with a clinking of chains and drawing of bolts, the door was opened. A tiny, white-haired woman in a dressing gown with skin like ancient parchment peered up at Crow through watery eyes. "What's the matter? What's all the banging about?" she squeaked.

"Matter? The matter is we're gettin' bombed by the Jerries missus and you've got the place lit up like a Christmas tree."

"What Christmas tree? It's not Christmas yet is it? I was sleeping, what's the time?" asked the old woman, drawing her gown tighter as she stared at the huge, alarming stranger blocking her doorway in the middle of the night.

Crow softened his voice. "Beg pardon if I scared you ma. But you've got a light showin' an' your curtains ain't shut as tight as they should be. Lights are not permitted during air raids. It's the law. I'm the Warden that enforces the law. Now I'll just switch off the light and sort your curtains for you. Then I'll be on my way an' you can get back to bed."

Brushing past the woman before she could object, Crow moved briskly through the small hall. "Just checking the lights dear," he called over his shoulder in the most soothing tone he could muster.

"You can't do this. You've no right," cried the old woman. "If my Bert was still alive he'd have you out on your ear you great lummox. I've a good mind to call the police."

Crow decided the gentle approach wasn't working. Spinning around and glaring down at her, he turned his voice up to full, foghorn volume. "You try to be nice to some people and what do you get? Nothin' but abuse for your trouble. Now listen 'ere missus. I am the police, or as good as where blackouts is concerned.

"It's my duty to uphold the law and I could, if I was nasty" - at this point he bent down and whispered in the woman's ear - "I could report you to the authorities for showin' a light an' then where would you be. Eh?"

The old woman's lip began to quiver.

"I'll tell you where you'd be – in court up on a charge an' liable for a heavy fine. Or if you couldn't afford to pay the fine" – and here Crow looked pointedly around the shabby hall with its worn carpet and scratched furniture and lowered his voice even further – "you would go to prison."

Tears coursed down the old woman's wrinkled face and she began to shake uncontrollably. "Prison." The awe and horror in her voice as she mouthed the word was so amusing to Crow he wanted to laugh - great gusts of rib-tickling, belly bursting laughter – right in her face. Instead he put a great beefy arm around her shoulders.

Her bones felt as brittle and small as a sparrow's. One twist and her scrawny neck would snap like a twig. Wouldn't that be nice. That crunching and mashing sound as her bones cracked, broke and turned to powder between his fingers. Hmm. The giant's thumbs began to itch and press deeper into her yellow, mouldy flesh.

Stop! The scream in his head had the power of an electric shock surging through his system. Think. Be clever. Do nothing dangerous. Nothing that could harm you, was the message his rusty brain received from that inner voice.

He heard himself speaking again – at first it sounded far away like when you're in the swimming pool and get water in your ears – and then the blockage cleared and his voice was back to normal.

"But none of that needs to happen," he was saying. "Nobody needs to hear about this. I won't say a word if you don't."

"Now let's get you tucked up in bed." Weeping quietly, the old woman allowed herself to be steered back to her bedroom. "There's the culprit," the giant crooned, switching off the bedside lamp. "Sweet dreams. Sleep tight, don't let the bed bugs bite. Don't worry, I'll let myself out."

Closing her bedroom door quietly, Crow moved quickly through the house.

His training with Bird flooded back to him as he searched. The main hiding places for valuables were usually the bedroom, bathroom, or kitchen. If she had picked the bedroom, well, his thumbs might have to start itching again. Deciding that he would cross that bridge if he had to come to it, he started in the toilet.

He found nothing in either the medicine cabinet, or behind the cistern and – holding his nose against the stink of the wee-stained carpet – got out as fast as possible.

Entering the darkened kitchen, he gasped again. If he had thought the smell from the toilet was bad, the stench in the kitchen was a hundred times worse. Poo, he thought as, ignoring the blackout regulations, he switched on the light.

At first, he couldn't see where the awful smell was coming from and then he almost tripped over it. A small chocolate brown Labrador puppy lay cowering behind a cupboard. It was shaking harder than the old woman and had done the toilet on the floor several times by the state of things. At that moment the explosion of another bomb shook the house, the lights above him shivered, and a cloud of dust fell from the ceiling. The dog's eyes rolled back in its head until only the whites were showing, it let out a pathetic whimper and, squatting on quivering legs, relieved itself again.

Taking a deep breath, Crow made a frantic search of the drawers and scanned the shelves. Just as he was about to release his breath and give up, his eyes fell on a red and gold tin sitting behind the tea-pot. "It's always in the tea pot, or under the biscuits," he gasped as the contents of his stomach struggled to cope with a fresh intake of putrid air.

Crow found the old woman's savings in the biscuit tin. A stream of sixpences, shillings, thrupenny bits, pennies and halfpennies fell on to the kitchen table. He assembled the coins into separate columns – counting each one greedily. At the end of his calculations, Crow's great shoulders slumped and he stared in disbelief at the money. "Two pound, fifteen shilling an' sixpence," he said. "This ain't fair. She must 'ave more."

Then the explanation dawned on him. It was as plain as the nose on his face, or more accurately, the horrible smell that was getting up his nose. "It's that damn dog. She spent the money on that bloody pup for company 'cos her darlin' Bert is pushin' up the daisies. The lousy, selfish old skinflint. I've a good mind to crush every bone in her rotten body." His hand hovered in the air about to sweep the money aside.

Then he got a better idea and, grunting, he shovelled the cash into his pocket instead. Grabbing the puppy by the collar, he held it at arm's length as he marched through the hall crashing the door behind him. "Not keen on fireworks or big bangs, eh dog. Well, never mind, you'll get used to it. Toilet training is what you need," he said, tossing the terrified animal into the gutter, before running up the street.

CHAPTER 29

In the months that followed Crow practised and gradually became more successful at robbing frightened old people living alone.

But the rewards of his crooked trade were slender – a few pounds stolen from a jam jar here, a few more pounds stolen from under a flower- pot there. It was very frustrating for someone as greedy as Crow. He was on the lookout for much bigger pickings – something that would have made his late, headless Uncle Bird proud of him. A real killing. And that is exactly what he found. Not that he immediately realised the fact.

"Crow," said the Chief Warden one morning after a particularly heavy air raid the night before, "I've got the ideal job for a big, strong lad like you. We need someone to help the rescue men."

The rescue men were teams of volunteers who had the dangerous and difficult job of searching through bombed buildings for survivors of the air raids. The problem was that most of the people they found were dead, so it would really have been more accurate to call the teams "recovery men" as it was mainly bodies they brought out of the rubble.

"Ideal" was not the word Crow would have used for his new job. London wasn't only dangerous during the air raids. The mornings following the nightly attacks were every bit as terrifying, when people emerged from their shelters to witness the awful destruction caused by the bombing. Fire and smoke filled the sky. And dust was everywhere – choking lungs, covering hair and clothes, even getting into the food that people ate.

Blackened and exhausted firemen were joined by teams of volunteers, who formed human chains passing buckets of water from hand to hand, in the bid to put out the towering flames.

Deep gaping holes, the size of ponds, pitted the roads causing traffic jams and making it difficult for fire engines and ambulances to get through to the injured.

Twisted and broken pipes spewed fountains of water, deadly amounts of gas leaked from other pipes, and electricity cables lay exposed, like giant lethal snakes, waiting for some poor unsuspecting person to trip and fall on them and then, sizzle, fry, and die in that horrifying order.

Then there were the unexploded bombs and mines hiding in the rubble, still alive, ticking quietly away, once more waiting for someone to put a foot wrong, step on them and KABOOM – be blown to smithereens.

But worst of all were the buildings that had been hit by the bombs. They were time- bombs too for the rescue men. Not one of the rescuers ever knew whether the floor he was walking on might suddenly open up, like the mouth of a hungry monster, sending him hurtling down to lie broken on the rubble below. At any moment the roof could collapse on his head, a falling beam could snap his neck, or a girder break his back. This was the death trap the Chief Warden had sent Crow into.

Although he was shaking in his size 18 boots, everyone around him showed enormous bravery getting on with the most dangerous jobs.

Even women risked their lives daily by driving ambulances through streets littered with potentially fatal hazards and past buildings teetering on the brink of collapse. So there was no way Crow could refuse to help and he could think of no excuse believable enough to allow him to back out.

There were, however, compensations that only someone as despicable as Crow would ever have thought of. As those around him fought to save the seriously injured from the rubble, Crow put on a great show of using his immense strength to heave the tonnes of bricks aside.

But as soon as he was sure everyone else was concentrating on saving the person, he would gradually fade to the back of the group and look for other less fortunate victims. If he was first to find a dead body buried in the rubble he could relieve them of their valuables before anyone else had a chance to check.

Watches were the easiest things to steal. It only took a matter of seconds to slip a nice gold or silver timepiece off a cold wrist and into his haversack. Jewellery took a bit longer because rings were often tight and he often had to break fingers to remove them. Frisking pockets was also time consuming, but the rewards – cash, valuable pens, and food coupons – were always worth the risk to Crow.

He was amazed at how much money many of the bodies had on them until he realised that people were carrying their life savings around. During peace-time they would have put their money in a bank, or kept it at home under the bed. But in a war like this no one could be sure that their house or bank would be standing the morning after an air raid.

Of course Crow didn't dare keep the horde on him. The penalties for looting were unmistakable and severe. Government notices posted all over London issued the following stark warning: *"Looting from premises that have been damaged by, or vacated by reason of war operations, is punishable by death or penal servitude for life."*

So every night he stashed his day's takings from the dead under a loose floor-board in the shed. His wealth grew quickly and he laughed hard and long when he realised that – no matter how smart Uncle Bird had thought himself to be – John Crow had proved to be smarter and richer.

Chapter 30

Like all downfalls, his came suddenly and unexpectedly out of a clear blue sky. Crow had wangled himself into a position where his fellow rescuers respected and trusted him for the seemingly heroic efforts he made to release the hundreds of injured from the rubble. Their trust increasingly allowed him more time to slip away on some excuse about helping the ambulance drivers or firemen. He used the time to search for more bodies and the booty they surrendered.

The only problem was that the people who lived in the East End were among the poorest in London and Crow was getting greedier. He wanted richer pickings, so he started wandering further away from his rescue team.

On one particularly sunny day he found himself in an elegant avenue of large houses that had been damaged by the bombing the night before. The street was empty and eerily quiet without even the sound of birdsong in the trees. The firemen had already reduced the fires to smouldering ash. The ambulances had ferried the dead and dying to hospital. They too were long gone. Everything that could be done in such a desperate time had been done.

Now, like hundreds of other neighbourhoods throughout the city, the place had been left to mourn, lick its wounds, and recover on its own.

Heartless as he was, even Crow couldn't fail to sense the feeling of sadness and loss which hung in the air as thick as the pall of black smoke rising from the ruined houses.

But he sensed something else when he saw the charred hulk of the once fine mansion. Sniffing the air like a bloodhound, he sensed that the firemen and rescue teams had left something behind. Something precious. His head swivelled round checking the street and the houses that still stood. No one on the pavement and no one that he could see behind the shattered windows – the bomb blasts had blown out the glass in every one. He moved carefully up the steps, testing each one to make sure it would take his weight.

The mansion was on three floors and peeled open to the sky, like a giant doll's house. Most of the furniture had been burned to a black crisp and was sodden and still steaming from the firemen's hoses. But the occasional chair, or table was recognisable and, beyond the smouldering stench, Crow smelled money. Someone rich had lived here.

He found the woman on the third floor under a wrought iron table by a window. She was completely unmarked and her beautiful face looked so peaceful, at first Crow thought she was asleep and caught himself asking out loud if she was all right. He cursed his stupidity. Of course she wasn't all right. She was as dead as a doornail. But just to make sure he moved her long brown hair aside to feel for the pulse in her neck.

For a second his breathing stopped. The swan-shaped neck was as cold as marble, but around it hung a necklace of glittering white diamonds.

"Oh God. My God. Rich. As rich as the finest gent in Mayfair, I'll be," cackled Crow, doing a jig of triumph on the floorboards until an ominous creak brought him back to his senses.

"Calm. Calm," he said, but his fingers shook uncontrollably as they felt for the clasp. It was small and intricate, fiddly, and he cursed as his thick, clumsy fingers failed to unlock the necklace.

Pulling the woman's head off the floor, he struggled and sweated, but the tiny hook evaded his efforts. With an exasperated roar, his mighty hands wrenched the neck around with a horrible grinding noise and he ripped the necklace away. He was blowing away the strands of fine brown hair that had become entwined in the clasp when a voice froze him to the spot.

"Put your hands above your head, get up, and turn around slowly." There was no mistaking the commanding tone. The voice belonged to someone in authority, someone used to being obeyed. Crow's giant frame shuddered as he turned and saw the soldier. In fact Crow could see from the man's helmet and the red armband that he was a special soldier called a Military Policeman. His gun pointed unwavering at Crow's stomach.

Even as he started trying to talk his way out of it, Crow knew he was in big trouble. "She's stone dead guv," Crow whimpered. "She must 'ave been overlooked what wiv all the smoke and everyfing."

"You didn't overlook her though did you? What's that in your hand? Bring it here, slowly."

The soldier's eyes hardened to match the icy glitter of the diamonds when he saw the necklace. "Robbing the dead. You fiend! he exclaimed, grabbing the necklace from Crow. "Stand over there where I can see you. If you so much as twitch, I'll shoot you," ordered the soldier as he knelt down and made a quick inspection of the body.

When he rose, his cheeks were flushed with anger. "This woman's neck's been broken. You murdered her and stole her jewellery – and you a warden. Someone in a position of trust – supposed to help people." The soldier shook his head in disbelief. His finger tightened on the trigger as he levelled the gun at Crow.

"No. No. Please," Crow begged falling to his knees. "I didn't do no killing. She were dead already. I found her that way."

"Her neck!" shouted the soldier. "I suppose her head twisted round on it's own."

"All right. Okay. I did steal the necklace. I couldn't get it off. She was already DEAD for pity's sake," weeped Crow.

The soldier's finger relaxed on the trigger as he appeared to come to a decision. "I'm not going to shoot you. A bullet's too quick for a coward like you. I intend to see you hang for this. But one false move and I'll finish it now. Now start walking."

The steel nozzle of the gun pressed hard against Crow's spine as he descended the stairs. He could see the soldier's jeep parked outside. How could he have failed to hear the man coming? But he knew the answer to that question only too well.

Pure greed. He had been completely obsessed with the diamonds. Another bomb could have fallen on the house and he wouldn't have noticed. Well, now he was going to pay for that greed, he thought miserably. Hung by the neck until his head flopped like the woman's and he was every bit as dead.

He desperately tried to think of a way out, but, as his Uncle Bird had always said, his brain was rusty, the cogs and wheels didn't move as fast as other people's. One thing he knew for certain. The man behind him was a brave, professional soldier. He had a gun and he undoubtedly both knew how to use it, and wouldn't hesitate if Crow tried any funny business. He was sunk – as deep and permanently as the Titanic.

Then something remarkable happened. One minute, the gun was jabbing painfully in his back, the next it was gone as Crow heard a loud splintering crack.

The giant turned to see – nothing at all. The soldier had disappeared into thin air. When he looked down he understood.

The step above him had given way and the soldier had fallen through the floor. It had happened so quickly that the man hadn't even had time to cry out.

Crow looked down through the gaping hole and saw the soldier lying among the rubble below. As he stared, the soldier groaned and attempted to move. Then Crow saw the gun lying within a few feet of the man. There wasn't a second to spare. Taking the collapsing steps three at a time, he bounded down the stairs.

He made it as the soldier's groping fingers were within inches of the gun. Kicking it fiercely away, the giant picked up a brick and without hesitation brought it down on the defenceless soldier's head. As he struck again and again, he remembered doing the same thing to a fox he had found injured in the road when he was a child.

When it was over and he was certain the soldier was dead, Crow reclaimed the necklace, took the man's belt and holster, and buried the body as deep as he could beneath the rubble.

Pausing only to pick up the gun, Crow ran from the house and past the jeep. It would only be a matter of time before the soldier's colleagues began searching for him. They would find his vehicle and then they would find him with his head caved in. Then they would be investigating the murder of a military policeman. Crow didn't want to be around when that happened.

As darkness fell and he hurried home through the East End, the air-raid sirens began their dervish wail. Minutes later the beams of a thousand search-lights criss-crossed the sky and he heard the familiar drone of enemy planes. This time though, the noise sounded deeper, denser, like a million angry bumble bees instead of a thousand.

Quickening his steps he turned into Solomon Street as the anti-aircraft guns opened fire and the first bombs started exploding. The last lap – five minutes and he would be home. He was more thankful for that thought than he had ever been. He had a bad feeling about this raid. Maybe it was what had happened earlier – the woman, and then the soldier – that was causing it. But Crow knew himself well enough to know that wasn't the main cause. Their innocent deaths were already a receding memory in his small, ant-like brain. His own brute instinct for survival was the reason for the sinking sensation in the pit of his stomach.

Others were sensing the same omens. There seemed to be a greater urgency in the movement of the few stragglers left in the streets. It never ceased to amaze someone as selfish as Crow how orderly and polite people usually were with each other even in the middle of an air raid when their lives were clearly in peril. So the sight of a crowd fighting to be first into an Underground station only served to emphasise his growing sense of unease. He had to move into the gutter to avoid an angry woman as she lashed out at a man with her umbrella. The man's response – a punch, which mashed her nose and knocked off her spectacles – was behaviour he had rarely seen in the Blitz.

The ground-shuddering thud of the bombs grew closer and Crow looked up to see the great cathedral of St Paul's ringed by a wall of fire. It was the middle of winter yet the air around him scorched his skin and was alive with jagged flying metal.

A taxi – its headlamps hooded and leaking baleful puddles of jaundiced light - came screeching round a corner and slewed to a halt opposite a terraced house further along the street. A soldier carrying a small girl with blonde ringlets got out. The driver dumped their bags on the pavement, took the fare without looking at it, and was off down the street before his passengers had rung the door-bell.

Crow automatically dodged into a doorway when he saw the uniform. He only got a glimpse of the slim blonde woman who opened the door, but the snapshot of joy on her face before they disappeared inside told him that her family had returned.

Crow wondered what that feeling of family would be like. How different might it have been for him if his mother had survived his birth and brought him up? He was still pondering that unanswerable question when the power of the blast threw him to the ground.

He rose slowly, as if in a trance, and shook a miniature storm of glass and dust from his hair and clothing. When he looked again the terraced house where the taxi had stopped was gone. In its place was an inferno of flames and collapsing masonry. For a second he thought he heard a scream above the roaring fire, and then the voice of a child weeping and crying for help.

He was a warden. It was his duty to rescue the dead and the dying. He knew that. But when had he ever done his duty? At that moment perhaps he screamed too. He never knew for sure and didn't think about it later. Instead, plugging his fingers in his ears, he ran as fast as his giant legs would carry him, and didn't stop running until he reached the wasteland that was Bird's Paraphernalia.

At the ruined gates he slumped to the ground exhausted, his great head drooping, eyes blinded by the sea of salty sweat coursing down his face. In this state, he sensed rather than saw that something was wrong. The whole of London seemed to be burning. Fifteen hundred separate fires had merged into two gigantic infernos turning the night sky red and threatening to consume the ancient city. But his face was suddenly fanned by the same burst of prickly heat that he had felt after the explosion in Solomon Street. And there were long, leaping shadows on the ground. Shadows at night was definitely wrong – far less long, leaping shadows. Crow's heart gave a sickening lurch as he squinted through tear-stained eyes at the bonfire that had been the shed.

"Nooooo" The giant's cry sounded like a mournful whale as he stumbled across the yard to the shed. He got to within two yards, but the licking flames drove him back and then, with a final groan, the roof collapsed. While the embers were still glowing red-hot, Crow scrabbled like a madman, screaming as he tore at the floor-boards and his hands burned. He found nothing for his extreme pains – except molten lumps that had once been gold rings and bundles of coal-black cinders that had once been bank notes. They crumbled in his tortured fingers.

Chapter 31

He fell asleep on the edge of his ruined home. Around midnight a thought stirred the fog of his misery and a glimmer of hope awakened him. His damaged fingers fumbled desperately through his haversack until at last they grasped the prize and he let out a ragged sigh of relief.

The Great Blitz had created its own necklace. A chain of fire encircled the city so that, no matter in which direction he looked, every horizon glowed blood-red in the darkness. Crow raised the diamonds to the skyline and fire washed through the stones making them so dazzlingly white that he had to shield his eyes against their brilliance.

"Twinkle, twinkle little star. How I wonder what you are… Diamonds," he giggled. "Sparklers that can still make me rich if I get things straight in my head and think my way out of this. But I got to think."

He looked around furtively, as if expecting to see a squadron of soldiers, or a posse of policemen surrounding the wasteground.

There was no one. Except for the ghost of Uncle Bird – and Crow scoffed at such a thought, once you was dead you was permanently pushin' up daisies in his book - Bird's Paraphernalia remained deserted.

But he knew that he had to move on – and quickly. Even being out on a night like this was suspicious, not to mention downright dangerous to a bloke's health.

The main priority was finding a new billet, somewhere to lay his head, until he could come up with a plan of what to do with the diamonds.

His bones ached with tiredness and he physically moaned at the effort of thinking. It would have to be somewhere very close, or he would fall asleep standing up. But where? Where in this godforsaken world of fire and bombs would he find such a place?

Like all the best ideas, it came to him when he had given up trying to think. Just popped quietly into his head without any fanfare or fuss when he thought his rusty brain had put the lights out for the night.

"The school." It was so perfect he said it out loud. It was just a couple of streets away. No one could possibly be around on an infernal night like this and he could even use one of them mats the brats did their gymnastics on as a bed. That would be every bit as comfortable as the mattress he had slept on in the shed.

It was pitch black by the time Crow arrived. The great fires were still raging all over the city, but somehow this street had escaped unscathed, and the crimson glow of distant infernos glimmered faintly behind the dark silhouette of the school.

The school was entirely open to entry. The six- foot high, spear-shaped railings had long since been torn from the low surrounding wall leaving a long row of ugly, toothless gaps in the stone. The gate was also missing. All the iron had been taken to be melted down and made into guns and planes for the war effort. So Crow simply walked in – or rather groped his way into the playground. Taking his bearings from the skeletal outline of a tree, he found the gym hall and then worked his way to the back of the building.

The toilet window was open, but he still had to smash the frame in order to squeeze his giant bulk through the space. Sweating and cursing from the effort, it took him five minutes and then he promptly put one massive boot down the WC. More oaths followed as he struggled to remove his soaking foot and trouser leg.

Groping his way from the toilet, he found the hall's swing doors and entered the gym. A sliver of fire-tinted light coming through high, narrow windows allowed him to make out the gym's familiar shapes.

In the middle of the hall he could see the trestle table, where he had tampered with the gas masks. Across the room the rows of cardboard coffins remained stacked against the wall bars. The vague, sweaty-leather smelling bulk of the vaulting horse was in one corner, while the large stores cupboard – containing all the PE equipment – was in the other.

He headed for the stores cupboard and after another wrestling match with medicine balls, skipping ropes, and an iron dumb-bell, which rolled off a shelf and set the giant cursing as it fell on to his dry foot, Crow found a mat and dragged it into the hall.

Grabbing a dusty canvas sheet as bedding from the vaulting horse, he finally collapsed with an exhausted sigh and was asleep before his head hit the gym mat.

He wasn't sure what woke him – the numbing chill of his wet foot, or the scraping sound. He wanted to think it was his freezing toes. More than that, he wanted to be sound asleep because – although his cold foot made him uncomfortable – the scraping sound raised the hair on his arms and at the base of his neck.

It wasn't loud and – for a moment – as he held his breath and listened in the darkness – he thought it had stopped. Then, just as he began to relax, ready to doze off, it happened again, slightly louder, marginally closer, and much scarier.

Inch by inch, he raised his head from the mat and peered into the darkness. In the far corner the vaulting horse looked to be in exactly the same position. The trestle table didn't appear to have moved. His eyes swept the floor for any sign of intruders. Rats! That was it. All the children had been evacuated, or taken out of school. The place was closed down until further notice, so it had to be vermin. The place must be infested with them. He shivered at the thought. It didn't make him feel much better, but at least he had solved the mystery. He felt for his gun and then changed his mind. Too noisy. Even in a blackout people might come looking if he started shooting. He would have to find something to batter them with instead if they got too close.

Grumbling with fatigue, he got up and started making his way towards the equipment store. Half way across the hall, he heard the scraping sound again. It was coming from the direction of the wall bars and the cardboard coffins. They were nesting in the coffins.

His hand closed around the butt of his revolver. Noise or not, he would take his chances and shoot the filthy things. He pushed the first stack over, ready to shoot at the first glimpse of fur or tail. He didn't quite make it to the second stack.

With a scraping sound he would remember until the day he was executed, the first cardboard coffin was pushed open and Crow saw a pale swan-like neck he recognised only too well. As her head turned on her shoulders to face him he heard the noise of grinding bones. Screaming, he pushed the lid shut and shoved the coffin over.

As it fell the lid of the second coffin in the stack flew open to reveal the military policeman – or what was left of him. All that Crow could identify was the man's peaked cap bearing the distinctive red badge. Any trace of a face beneath had disappeared in a mash of blood and bone. Yet when he looked closely and - much as he desperately wanted to he could not pull his eyes away – he saw traces of brick dust in the smashed teeth and then the burst lips peeled back to repeat the following phrase. "Looters are hung by the neck until they are dead. Looters are hung by the neck until they are dead. Looters are hung by the neck until they are dead."

Crow stood rooted to the spot, like a rabbit caught in a car's headlights, hypnotised by the apparition and its awful message. Only when the coffin started to fall towards him was the trance broken and he threw himself aside with a yelp of terror. It missed by inches, but he was certain a dead hand had grasped at his clothing as he scrabbled across the floor and dived under the trestle table.

He found the gun was still in his hand, but it shook so much that he could not raise it to aim and, anyway, what good were bullets against ghosts. Trembling under the table, he could see no trace of them. Perhaps they were gone? Maybe they had never been there in the first place. He was probably still asleep. That was it. He was fast asleep and experiencing a very realistic nightmare.

Then the lid of the third coffin flew open and Crow screamed again. Eyes on stalks, he stared through the darkness at the interior bracing himself for the horror.

But there was nothing there. No mouldering body. The cardboard coffin was empty. His ragged sobs of relief caught in his throat when he heard another sound.

Something was rolling across the floor. He strained to identify the sound. Well, whatever it was wasn't rolling, like say a medicine ball, or a football would roll. It wasn't the smooth, uninterrupted sound that a perfectly round object would make. Every so often the rhythm of the roll was interrupted by a slight bump. The sort of bump something round with an uneven surface would make – like a hand grenade.

He sat up straight and gripped one of the table legs. But wait. The noise a rolling hand grenade would make would be clicking, metallic. This sound was softer, squishier. Then the sound stopped – and the soft squishy thing bumped gently into the back of Crow's hand.

He leapt in the air bouncing his head off the underside of the table. As the pain shot through his brain, he remembered where he had heard the sound before and felt a warm, damp patch spread down his trousers as he wet himself.

On the floor beside him the severed head of Uncle Bird spoke in the darkness. "Spare the rod, spoil the child. Idle hands make mischief." Crow could hear his uncle's laughter ringing in his ears as he sprinted from the school playground.

CHAPTER 32

Dawn had yet to break upon the devastated city, but the railway station was a heaving mass of people, queuing for tickets at the wooden booths, waiting patiently under the hand-written cardboard signs advertising "Air Raid breakfasts, 6am – served from 1/8d", or simply sitting exhausted on battered suitcases.

To Crow's bleary eyes - as he used his haversack as a cushion on the cold stone floor - it looked as though half of London was attempting to escape the city. He certainly was. If they hadn't already done so, the rescue team would soon report him missing. In the same way a search would be launched for the military policeman. It would only be a matter of time before his jeep was spotted and the body turned up. Crow shuddered as the image of the soldier's crushed face leapt unbidden into his brain. Then the authorities might put two and two together. He didn't want to be there when they did. What with the Blitz, the murder, and now literally seeing things that went bump in the night (he shivered again at the thought of Uncle Bird's disembodied head) the Big Smoke had literally become too hot for comfort. This was his last chance to get out and make a new start somewhere with his new found wealth.

Crow was patting the reassuring bump the diamond necklace made in his haversack when a hand fell on his shoulder. "Blimey mate. You're not 'alf jumpy. Anyone would think you'd stolen the crown jewels."

The policeman standing before Crow had a beaming, round face and a pleasantly plump frame to go with it. No one looking at the officer would have dreamt for a second that there was a war on, far less that strict food rationing applied.

But Crow's yammering heart slowed down a fraction. Even he knew that policemen – even terminally jolly policemen - did not customarily appear so cheerful when about to arrest someone on a murder charge. However, he did not trust his voice to remain calm. So he cracked his face into a smile and waited silently for what was to come.

"The truth of it is, we've got a bit of a problem here and you could help out, being a warden and all." The policemen stood grinning as he appraised Crow's uniform and, dusting himself down, Crow rose smartly to his feet.

"Oh. Of course officer. Anythin' I can do. It's been a bit of a long night. That's all." The policeman nodded sympathetically. "Know what you mean. Just heard the wireless before I left the station. They're saying that Jerry gave us the worst poundin' of the war last night. East End's been knocked flat. Paternoster Street took the brunt of it. Somehow St Paul's escaped. Gawd knows how. He must look after his own," said the policeman, raising his eyes to the station's great cathedral- like ceiling. "Anyway, the thing is, I'm in charge of this group of tiddlers."

His helmet nodded in the direction of a ragged tribe of children. None of them looked older than seven. They were dressed in one of two colours – drab grey, or drab brown – and surrounded by a sea of make-shift luggage, ranging from small brown suitcases to overstuffed hold-alls and khaki haversacks just like Crow's. A smattering of toy buckets and spades provided the only splash of brightness. Like Paddington Bear, all of them wore luggage labels bearing their names and addresses – and every one carried a large cardboard box dangling from a piece of string around their necks. The boxes contained their gas masks. Most of them looked on the verge of tears and some had already given in, blowing their noses on dirty white and brown chequered handkerchiefs.

"They're to be evacuated first thing this morning," said the policeman. "Only problem is their billeting officer hasn't turned up."

"Billeting officer?" Crow looked blankly at the policeman.

"You know – the warden that takes 'em on the train and makes sure they get billeted safe and sound."

Understanding – and then the realisation of a great opportunity – began to dawn on Crow and he had to stifle the huge grin that threatened to crease his face from ear to ear. The policeman was still talking and Crow's great brow furrowed in concentration. "Only thing I can think of is that the poor blighter copped it last night during the bombing."

"What about their parents?" asked Crow.

Laughing, the policeman removed his helmet and scratched his bald head. "How long have you been a warden? Don't you know the rules? No parents allowed in the station. Upsetting enough as it is. With mums and dads sobbin' their eyes out, nobody would ever get anywhere. Anyway, look I got to get back to the station and these tiddlers have got to get to Brighton. Can you take 'em?"

Which was how John Crow found himself leading a crocodile line of small children along platform 13 at Victoria Station. He watched the steam rising in giant cigar-shaped whorls from the funnel of the idling black engine towards the glass dome and allowed himself to dream.

This was his ticket to freedom. The way he was going to escape his old, miserable existence in the grime of the city and begin a new, wealthy life in the country. He would be a gentleman of leisure on the proceeds of the necklace. But first he was going to have to get rid of the band of snivelling brats he had inherited.

As if to remind him, he felt a tug on his sleeve and looked down to see a tiny, pale face with startlingly large brown eyes staring intently up at him. In one hand the little girl clutched a balding teddy bear missing an ear. Her other gripped an equally small blonde classmate as though their lives depended upon it.

"Please Mister we need to go," they trilled in perfect unison.

"Yes, yes. We'll all be goin' in a minute. You need to be patient. Like all the other brats," he hissed under his breath.

"No Mister, you don't understand," piped up brown eyes. "Not go on the train. Go! Me friend Dolly an' me need to go to the toilet."

"Look. Can't you just hold on for a couple of minutes? Til we get on board."

Dolly's face pinched and she wailed. "Mary, I swear, I'll do it in me knickers if we don't go this minute."

Crow flinched at the sobbing. How could such a tiny creature make so much noise, he wondered. But her crying was drawing too much attention for his liking. The commotion was causing people to turn and stare. The last thing he wanted was an audience.

"All right little girls," he said, forcing himself to pat Mary's head when crushing it would have been so much more satisfying. "Of course you can go to the toilet, but please hurry. Suddenly a forest of hands shot up repeating the same chorus. "Please Mister, can we go to the toilet too."

Crow heard the piercing whistle as he stamped impatiently up and down outside the toilets. He rushed back on to the platform in time to see the guard furling up his red flag as the Brighton train chugged out of the station.

"Hey. Hey. That's our train. We're supposed to be on that train. Can't you do something? Blow your whistle," shouted Crow, waving his arms as he ran along the platform towards the guard. Too late now my old son. Never mind, there'll be another one along in a couple of hours," the man said cheerfully.

Crow wanted to ram the guard's whistle down his throat. Two hours was a lifetime. For all he knew the authorities might be hot on his trail. He looked wildly around the station. There were far too many soldiers and policemen on the platforms for his liking. He could be facing arrest at any minute and after that the game would be up. A military trial. A guilty verdict – and then a short, sharp drop at the end of a rope. He gulped. The mere thought of it made him break out in a cold sweat. He dare not stay in London a minute longer. He had to be out of the city on the next train – and the brats were the perfect cover.

He hurried back to the toilets to find the last of the children emerging hand in hand. "All right. We missed our train, but we can catch another one and it won't make no difference," he crooned. He looked up at the big notice board showing departures and saw that the next train was due to leave in five minutes for a place called Horsham. The fact that it was going nowhere near Brighton didn't matter a hoot to Crow. What did he care where these brats ended up? Anyway, whose fault was it that they had missed the train? Theirs, not his. In fact, the more he thought about it the angrier he became. He was in increasing danger of being caught and hanged because these snivelling wretches couldn't hold on for a couple of minutes before they spent a penny. How unfair was that? Well they needed to be taught a lesson. He would get them so lost they might never see their parents again.

"While we wait for the next train why don't we play a game children?" A hundred small faces looked up at Crow expectantly. "What kinda game Mister?" piped up a cheeky voice from the back. "It's called the name-swopping game," said Crow. "What you do is swap your name and address labels with your best chum an' then mum's the word til I tell you to swap 'em back again. Right, start the swop."

Chapter 33

By the time the group boarded the Horsham train every label had been swapped and Crow was grinning with satisfaction at the chaos that would follow when the children were finally found in the wrong town wearing the wrong names.

A drizzle began to fall as the train clattered over the Thames and away from the capital. Ignoring the unwashed smells and early morning farts of the brats around him, Crow gazed at the small rivulets streaming down the carriage window and dreamed of his new life.

Gradually, through the skein of rain, he became aware of other shapes – ominously familiar shapes – floating high above the river. In that moment he was transported back in time and became a terrified child again cowering in the shed at Bird's Paraphernalia. "Zeppelins! We're under attack!" he yelped, automatically ducking into the seat and waiting for the explosions.

But there were no explosions and no mass panic. Only a warm female chuckle filled the silence as he slowly raised his head. Across the aisle beyond the gaping faces of the children sat the owner of the laugh. "They're not Zeppelins luvvie," said the old woman. "You're gettin' confused. Zeppelins was in the Great War. These are ours. Barrage balloons to protect us from the Jerries. There's nothin' to worry about."

He felt his neck and then his face prickle with the crimson heat of shame and he could only nod agreement.

They chugged past Battersea Power Station – its towering chimneys looming grey and menacing in the half- light. At Clapham Junction and Balham stations the train stopped to take on more evacuees for the countryside. The train overflowed with children, their toys and their tiny bundles of luggage. They all looked scared, but not half as scared as the giant who sat miserably among them.

After Hackbridge, Crow ceased to recognise any of the station names they passed. He was only fifteen miles away from London but could have been in a foreign country for all the villages of Wallington, Waddon, or Carshalton meant to him.

At Sutton the train stopped for almost an hour before a guard and three policemen walked along the platform. Heart beating frantically, Crow watched the men split up and climb aboard the carriages.

The bodies had been discovered. The manhunt was on. He was trapped. They were coming for him and there was nothing he could do - unless. He looked around. The old woman was still sitting in the aisle over from him and, of course, he was surrounded by the children.

What if he took a hostage? The old woman would be easier to handle, whereas children kicked and screamed, were sick and wet themselves. On the other hand, a child was more valuable than a wrinkly old crone. The coppers might think twice and back off if a brat's life was at risk. Brown eyes, the girl who started it all by needing to spend a penny, was sitting directly opposite hugging her moth-eaten teddy. He only needed to stretch across and grab her. He was preparing to do just that when the guard entered the carriage.

"Sorry about the delay everybody," he said. Crow's fingers dug into the armrest of his seat. "But you're all going to have to get off the train I'm afraid." The groan from the few adults in the carriage was drowned out by the cheer from the children.

The giant tensed himself preparing to leap for the girl. "There's a mechanical fault with the train, so it's being taken out of service. We'll get a replacement as soon as possible, but meantime you're all going to have to be patient."

The adults groaned louder, but Crow heaved a sigh of relief and almost had a spring in his step as got off the train.

Five hours later his relief had turned to frustration as he waited on the packed platform. When the replacement train finally arrived darkness was beginning to fall. Everyone climbed gratefully aboard again, but the journey had barely commenced when the familiar sound of air-raid sirens rent the air.

"Gawd they're startin' early tonight," the old woman said matter-of-factly between mouthfuls of corned beef sandwich.

Crow stared at her. The mad old witch hardly seemed concerned about the fact that the skies were about to come alive with enemy planes dropping hundreds of tonnes of lethal explosives on their heads.

Peering out the carriage window Crow saw a series of orange flashes illuminate the darkness as the first bombs fell on London. As he looked the flashes seemed to grow bigger and closer.

There was a long, low whistle, which finally grew piercingly loud and ended in a bright ball of fire when a bomb erupted in a field less than a hundred yards from the railway line. Crow felt the carriage rock and children screamed accompanied by the noise of shattering glass further down the train.

Suddenly the carriage lights went out, accompanied by the pandemonium of weeping children and adult voices on the edge of panic. The engine, which had travelled no more than a mile, slowed, limped along at a snail's pace, and then shuddered to a halt in a dimly lit station. Crow glimpsed the name Banstead on a small sign at the end of the platform.

Banstead it was then. Time to bale out. He groped in the darkness until his hands found the comfort of the haversack. Then he rose and began pushing his way through the blubbering children when a hand caught his sleeve.

"Where are you going?" In the meagre light afforded by the station platform, Crow made out the shape of the old woman. "It's alright ma. Nothin' to worry about. We'll need to get these tiddlers organised. Me an' the guard 'ill sort it out."

Crow tried to ease away, but the old woman grabbed his arm. "No you're not. You're a coward. I seen it in you this morning over the barrage balloons.

But these children need you mister. Their parents ain't here to look after em. That's your job now. You can't just run away and leave 'em."

Crow hesitated. She was right. He thought of all the people he had robbed, the dead woman, the Military Policeman, the girl with the ringlets. She had cried out for help. He should have gone to her. He should have helped her. Now here was a chance at least go some way to making up for the terrible things he had done in his life.

Then he remembered the dead woman's neck. That's how his neck would look with the hangman's noose around it. No amount of helping these children would save him from that fate. Shrugging the old woman off, he pushed out of the carriage door and ran along the platform away from her accusing cries.

His aim was to get as far away from the scene of his desertion and other people as quickly as possible. Directly outside the station Crow found a quiet path leading through woods. It seemed to head away from the village and he hurried along the meandering, uphill route accompanied by the distant crump of bombs as the air-raid grew in intensity.

After about half a mile, the wood ended and he emerged on to a long straight avenue, lined with pine trees. The street was a cul-de-sac ending in parkland on his right with a row of cottages on his left. He reckoned there was far less risk of encountering somebody in the park than on the street. But before he went towards the tiny playground, he stopped under a solitary gas lamp for another glimpse of his treasure.

He was near exhaustion and his burned fingers struggled with haversack catches which seemed peculiarly unfamiliar, but he eventually fumbled the flap open and groped inside for the necklace.

His fingers found nothing but strangely soft objects. He emptied the haversack under the gaslight and fell to his knees weeping in despair as he gazed upon the small pile of clothes – grey school shorts, a grey jumper, underwear, socks, a comb, toothbrush, and a threadbare teddy with one glass eye.

He had no idea how long he stayed there, but when John Crow finally regained his senses, his attention was drawn by a pale yellow storm lamp winking at him through the trees.

At first he stared dully without any understanding or thought at the light. But slowly, the fury grew in him until it reached boiling point.

There was a light on. Someone had a light on during an air-raid. Well, he was the Warden and it was his job, no his sworn duty, to enforce blackout regulations. Adjusting the holstered revolver at his waist, he strode towards Tumble Cottage as the first spluttering cough of a dying engine filled the night sky.

PART 4

Countdown

CHAPTER 34

Alex woke with a start. The chimes were jangling and dancing on her bed-side table as if they were being plucked by the invisible hand of a frenzied puppeteer.

She lay still, watching the slim pieces of metal collide and remembered Mum telling her that she had bought them in an American city called San Francisco during what she described with a giggle as her "hippy period - long before any of you lot were born."

The thought made Alex feel better, but only a little bit, and nowhere near good enough to start giggling. She looked beyond the chimes along the wire, which disappeared out her open window and snaked down the garden. It was thrumming gently as if live electricity was running through it. From her science lessons at St Oliphants she knew that couldn't be true. It was just a plain old wire with nothing alive in it – or at the end of it? Right? Alex listened intently to the noises outside in the darkness. Was that wind she heard blowing in the branches? Nothing. The night was perfectly still. Not even the hoot of an owl, or the scream of fighting cats broke the silence. For some unaccountable reason the phrase – "the calm before the storm" – ran through her head.

The chimes stopped. Slowly she lay down again, keeping her gaze fixed on them, willing them to stay still. They hung motionless. It was only an animal, she thought. An animal tripped the wire. Her eyelids drooped. Her head nodded and fell into the soft luxury of the pillow. Tinkling. The tinkling invaded her sleeping brain like the sound of a thousand tiny cymbals being crashed together by a fairy orchestra. Alex curled into a ball under the bedclothes and shut her eyes tighter, willing the metal storm away. But she knew it was hopeless. The chimes were dancing again and, if anything, they seemed more insistent than ever.

With an exhausted groan, she threw her duvet aside and got up.

Perhaps the foxes had returned, she thought as she put on her dressing gown. They could be chewing the wire just as they had chewed through a skipping rope Corker had left in the garden overnight a couple of weeks earlier. All that tugging and shaking of their heads would set up a fierce commotion in the wire. Enough to have the chimes jigging like wild dervishes. One thing Alex was certain of. She wouldn't get a wink of sleep until she went outside to investigate. Another thing she was equally sure about was that she wasn't going alone.

The difference hit her the minute she stepped on to the landing. The hall was colder, much colder than her bedroom. In fact it was like a refrigerator out here and the temperature was growing chillier as she moved along the landing towards the twins' bedroom. She could see her breath frosting on the air and drew her gown tighter.

The heating must have broken down she reasoned, automatically brushing the radiator with her fingers. She drew them away fast with a stifled yelp. The radiator was piping hot.

Her hand closed on the handle of the twins' door - and this time she could not stop the cry of surprise and pain that rose in her throat.

It was stuck, glued to the handle. Or, more accurately, her fingers were frozen to the handle in a grip of ice. First, she felt her hand go numb with the sort of feeling you get when you hold a snowball too long.

Then the burning sensation started. Fighting her rising panic, Alex brought her other hand on to the stuck one and pulled with all her strength.

With a horrible sucking, unsticking sound the skin of the stuck hand broke free from the handle and Alex sat down hard, smacking her back against the balcony. Cradling her throbbing hand under her armpit, like a bird with a broken wing, she sat blinking through watery eyes at the twins' door.

At first Alex couldn't believe what she was seeing. The lock inside the empty keyhole appeared to be turning on its own. Shaking the tears away, she stared harder at the keyhole. Yes. There was no doubt about it. Like the chambers of a sixgun – a gun like the Warden's was the crazy thought that flashed through Alex's head – the lock inside the keyhole was clicking round. One….two…three… four…

Pulling the sleeve of her dressing gown down over her uninjured hand, Alex made a desperate leap for the handle. Her protected fingers closed around the handle and pushed down hard on the stroke of the sixth click. But it was too late. With a final click that sounded deafening in Alex's ears the door locked and the twins' were imprisoned in the bedroom.

CHAPTER 35

"Alex, the door's stuck. We can't get out." Suddenly hearing Corker's terrified voice only inches away made me jump with fright. "How did you know I was at the door Corker," I asked feeling the cold on the landing seeping into my bones.

"I saw the chimes dancing and you getting up," she said as matter-of-factly as one might read a bus timetable.

"Okay," I said, hoping my voice still sounded normal. "You're right Corks, the door does seem to be stuck and I can't open it from the outside either. Is Jamie awake?"

"Yes. He was sleeping. But I spoke to him a minute ago in his head.
He's wakening up now."

It was getting even chillier in the hall. The questions could wait until later. Something told me the twins' were in grave danger and we were running out of time. I had to be brave for them and get on with it.

"All right Corks. Here is what we are going to do. I'm going to go outside to the patio. You and Jamie get over to the window and I'll tell you what to do from there."

With Corker's plaintive "hurree" echoing in my ears, I dashed downstairs and out through the French Windows. Looking up I saw the twins' faces looking pale and fearful as they pressed against their window and anger surged through me.

Whatever was doing this had no right to terrify my brother and sister.

I was determined to fight it to the end.

"Jamie, open the small window at the side," I called, signalling my instructions with my arms. "Okay, listen closely. I don't think we have much time. Open the large window in the middle now. That's it.

Now I want you both to take the sheets off your beds and, Jamie, tie them together using your best scout knots." Their heads disappeared from the window and I heard the swish and rustle of bedclothes being pulled from beneath mattresses.

Then I heard another noise, one that I would not have recognised had it not been so recently familiar. The click was quiet. It sounded almost sly, as if invisible creeping fingers wanted their work to go unnoticed until it was too late. It came from one of the small, upper windows already closed on the right hand side. Seconds later the mechanical clicking started on the larger closed window beneath.

"Jamie!" I screamed, "the windows are locking."

Snap! The small window Jamie had opened, shut and the lock clicked in one flashing movement. "Jamie stop the big window from closing," I yelled and he threw his shoulder against the window just in time. But I could see that my little brother was fighting a losing battle against the invisible force that was attempting to push the window closed.

Soon his strength would give out and the window would snap shut locking them both in the room.

"The baseball bat, Corker. Get Jamie's baseball bat. It's under his bed." Corker had never moved so fast in her life and within seconds was back at the window with Jamie's aluminium baseball bat.

"Now Corker, give the bat to Jamie. That's right. Jamie wedge the bat in the window frame." With the dying ounces of his strength Jamie jammed his bat in the window and slumped beneath my sight.

"Corker! What's happened to Jamie?"

"He's lying down," she answered as I saw the baseball bat quivering with tension in the window.

"Kick him! Get him up right now!" I commanded and I heard Jamie yelp in anger as Corker carried out my instruction.

Seconds later his head appeared over the window sill again.

"Quick," I ordered. Tie one end of the sheet to the handle of your sock drawer and throw the other end out the window."

One look at the trembling bat was enough for Jamie and he dived into action. "Okay Corks climb down. Don't worry, I'll catch you."

Without hesitation Corker clambered over the sill and began her descent down the bedsheet. The sheet was about four feet short of the patio. But when Corker reached the bottom she simply let herself drop and I managed to catch her legs and break her fall.

"Now you Jamie. Hurry," I shouted and he came fast hand over hand down the billowing sheet. Despite his speed, he was only half way down when there was a piercing crack and the bat exploded into a thousand pieces. The window snapped shut, followed by a final click that sounded to me as loud as a shotgun.

The sheet shot upwards and Jamie jumped clear of the patio landing with a mighty splosh in a giant snowdrift.

CHAPTER 36

Jamie emerged from the drift backwards in his usual mix'n'match nightwear. First his Simpson's slippers appeared. Followed by his tartan pyjama bottoms. Then the Action Man top. And finally the back of his head, spluttering and shaking the snow from his hair. But, apart from looking like a Yeti, he was unhurt. As we gradually recovered our senses, I became aware of the blue light once more shimmering faintly through the trees.

The others didn't need telling. It drew us like a magnet and I could feel the anger welling up inside me again. Something had invaded our garden. It had no right to be there and the three of us were going to see it off.

We were half way down the second section when Corker let out a blood-curdling shriek. I followed the direction of her shaking finger and saw a pair of yellow eyes glaring from the middle of a rhododendron bush.

Before Jamie or I could scream, the eyes shot from the bush attached to a ball of spikey, hissing fur.

"Noodles. It's Skankie's cat Noodles," I gasped as the relief flooded through me.

"He must have tripped the wire and set the chimes off," said Jamie. "Maybe he hurt his paw on it. He doesn't look too happy," he added.

Jamie was right. Noodles had stopped in the centre of the garden. His back was still arched and his unblinking eyes remained fixed on us.

Seeming completely unaware of Noodle's mood, Corker was approaching the cat with her hand out ready to pat him. "Here, Noodles. Here, nice kitty."

"That's not a good idea Corks," I warned moving to cut her off. The instant I moved, Noodles shot across to the other side of the garden disappearing into the bushes in a boiling froth of fur and spit.

"Heck. What rattled his cage!" exclaimed Corker and we all laughed nervously.

The voice cut through the stillness of the night stopping us dead in our tracks. It came from the beyond the holly bush in the same direction as the blue light. It sounded slightly posh and very bossy and certainly angry. But there was a fuzzy noise behind the voice and the words it spoke didn't make any sense. Here's what we heard:

"We shall fight on the beaches, we shall fight on the landing grounds, we shall fight in the fields and the streets, we shall fight in the hills; we shall never surrender...."

"That's not a real person," declared Jamie.

"Sshh, keep your voice down, or he'll hear us," I whispered. "What do you mean, it's not a real person?"

"I mean it's not a live person. You hear that hissing sound in the background? That's the noise a TV makes when its recording. The man's on TV."

The voice was still droning on and as I listened, I had to agree with Jamie. The voice did sound recorded.

I was completely bewildered. None of this made any sense. It was too crazy to understand. But we had to get to the bottom of it. I looked at my brother and sister and they nodded their heads in silent agreement.

We locked hands and went round the holly bush to face the unknown together.

The instant we stepped into the third section the blue light disappeared and the voice cut off.

But in the last fading rays of the light I saw the boy. He was at the entrance to the shelter. His back was to me and he was wearing what looked like a woollen helmet and shorts revealing long skinny legs. He was bending over something and as we emerged he half turned his head and I glimpsed the profile of a pale, desperately sad looking face. In that instant the light died completely and the boy vanished.

"I wish I had my baseball bat," whispered Jamie and I felt him shiver beside me. "Who...who is that boy, Alex?" asked Corker in a timid voice I had never heard coming from my little sister.

"I don't know," I said, knowing that the answer wasn't quite true. Deep down inside me a vague memory was stirring, but I wanted it to go away. I didn't want to remember where I had seen that pale face before.

"Let's find him," said Jamie and he marched over to the shelter. "All for one," I muttered. "And one for all," finished Corker and, hand in hand, we followed our brother.

There was no sign of the boy. We searched the bushes, behind the shed and went right along the school fence as far as the fox hole.

But it was as if he had vanished into thin air. We gathered together again at the spot where we had first seen him, stamping our feet to keep warm. There was a scraping sound as Jamie's foot made contact with something. He squatted down patting the snow and came up with what looked like a small black box. Then he turned it around and I felt my heart lurch in my chest. "Look Alex, it's the radio you and Mum found," he said.

"The boy must have turned it off," I heard myself say. But it was like someone else speaking underwater from far away.

"Well it doesn't work now," said Jamie, twiddling the knobs. "Maybe it needs new batteries."

"I don't think this radio needs batteries," I replied feeling dizzy again. "But what's it doing here?" asked Jamie, "I thought Mum put it in the loft with the other things?"

There was no logical answer to that question. All of us knew it, even Jamie. I looked across at Corker. She was beginning to sway. Even in the darkness I could tell she was chalk white.

"Come on Jamie," I said. "No more questions. We must get back to the house. Corker's had enough. She's exhausted."

Supporting Corker's arms between us, we retraced our footsteps on the crazy paving.

"One things for sure," said Jamie, as he stroked Corker's drooping head. "Noodles didn't trip the wire. It must have been the boy."

For a fleeting second a watery moon broke through the clouds and I saw the small black cross lying in the snow by the side of the path, as though someone in a hurry had dropped it. I picked it up, dusting the snow from the ribbon, and wondered how on earth the medal I had last seen on a shelf in Skankie's hallway had found its way into our garden?

CHAPTER 37

The hall was decked with yellow, red, and purple paper chains we had glued together ourselves. The walls of the little lounge were plastered with 105 cards. Corker had counted them all twice to make sure. The mantelpieces in every room were adorned with tinsel, candles, and Yule logs - home-made from papier-mache and painted brown like the ones we had seen on Blue Peter.

There were two Christmas trees. One inside, already surrounded by all shapes and sizes of exciting and mysterious gift-wrapped presents from our relatives.

And a bigger one in the garden. As darkness fell Mum performed the switching-on ceremony and we all gazed through the frosted glass of the French Windows at the white lights glittering outside.

Now Mum was busy in the kitchen preparing the meal for the big day. The delicious smell of her home-made lasagne wafted through the house, accompanied by the sound of her favourite classical music, something entitled Claire de Lune by a famous composer called Debussy.

Meanwhile, Dad was doing what he did best. The sound of his snoring rippled through from the big lounge. He was relaxing on the red and white striped sofa after a few beers, while an old black and white movie about Christmas and a giant invisible rabbit called Harvey flickered soundlessly on the TV in the corner.

The afternoon of Christmas Eve and everything appeared perfect in the Madden household.

Dad snoozing. Mum cooking. Santa and his reindeer getting ready for the biggest and most important delivery round of the year. Peace and goodwill to all men, women, and children on planet earth.

Only appearances can be very deceptive. Corker, Jamie and I couldn'tquite get into the Christmas spirit for the feeling that something amazing was going to happen. And we were not thinking about photographic evidence of Santa and the slay landing on our roof.

Our thoughts were much less pleasant than that. The signs had been building up over the past few nights. First, the appearance of the mysterious blue light. Then the foxes disappearing and the sound of the baby crying. The shadow of the woman in the garden. The shawl with the unknown initials RT. The appearance of the giant Warden. The terrifying invisible force that tried to lock the twins' in their bedroom. Broken old radios coming to life and playing at the bottom of the garden in the middle of the night. The mysterious lanky boy with the sad face. And now my latest discovery – Skankie's marathon medal lying abandoned in the snow at the side of our path, instead of where it should be, sitting on a shelf in the old man's house.

I had the feeling that things were getting way beyond our control. That we needed some adult advice. After a brief summit conference with the twins' we decided that we should at least approach Dad about the medal. We agreed that there was no way we could tell him the whole story. Grown-ups, particularly my parents, spook too easy. So we would simply miss out the strange bits.

"What whopping snorts," giggled Jamie as we entered the big lounge. Dad was still snoring fit to raise the rafters, so we tip-toed across to the settee and I gave his shoulder a gentle shake.

"Whoa… What's the matter? Your mother need my help in the kitchen?" he said, sitting up with a start and knocking his glass over.

"Aaargh! Alex. Now look what you've made me do. Your mother will skin me alive. Quick, get a cloth before the beer soaks into the new carpet."

Mopping up the puddle of lager, I realised that maybe now wasn't the best time to enlist Dad's help. But before I could beat a diplomatic retreat, Jamie had produced the medal.

"What's this then?" said Dad, still grumpy but quickly becoming intrigued as he surveyed the cross in Jamie's hand.

"It's a ...." Jamie began. "It's a marathon medal like Mum's," I interrupted quickly in case that well known blabber-mouth my little brother said too much. "We found it in the snow on the pavement just outside our front door. We've no idea how it got there Dad.

Have you seen anything like it?"

Dad sat up straighter, burped, and took the medal. He studied it for several minutes, turning it over in his hands before looking at Jamie suspiciously. "Now tell me the truth Jamie. Did you swop this with one of your mate's at school?"

"No Dad," squealed Jamie indignantly. "It's like Alex says. We found it in the snow outside. Honest."

"Okay. All I'm saying is that if you did, say so now, because this could be valuable to someone."

Jamie gave a fierce head shake and put on his scowling duck face.

"All right," said Dad seeming to come to a decision. Getting up, he switched off the black and white movie about the giant invisible rabbit, and moved purposefully towards the door.

"I'll tell you one thing Alex," he said as he left the room. "This medal has nothing to do with running races. It's far more important than that."

Half an hour later Dad emerged from the study clutching several pages of printed paper and called us back into the big lounge.

"Well, I don't know how this medal came to be outside our door," he began, "but it was once worn by a very brave man."

"Who Dad?" piped up Jamie.

"A German called Hans Baumer. I cleaned off some of the black dirt ingrained on the back of the medal and his name was there. See."

Dad held up the cross and the three of us examined the name printed in tiny letters on the back. "He was a World War I German air ace," said Dad filling in our awe-struck silence.

"What's that?" asked Corker.

"A champion plane shooter," sneered Jamie. "How many do you think he got Dad? Hey, wait a minute. The Germans were the enemy. How could they be brave. How could he win a medal?"

"Slow up Jamie, said Dad half smiling "and don't be so horrible to your sister. "I don't know how many planes he shot down. But I do know that he was brave. He had to be to win this medal. It is called the Order of Merit. I found out a bit about it on the internet. Shall I read it to you?"

We nodded and this is what he read: *"Established in 1667 by King Frederick I of Prussia, the Orden Pour le Merite was originally known as the Order of Generosity and awarded to military personnel and civilians. During World War I, Prussia's highest military award, the Orden Pour le Merite, was awarded to military personnel for repeated and continual gallantry. Recipients were required to wear the medal whenever they were in uniform.*

Of all officers in the German army and navy, the most frequent recipients of the Orden Pour le Merite were junior officers in the German Air Force. During World War I, it was awarded to 81 German military Aviators, 76 army aviators and five naval aviators. Of that total, 78 of the recipients were officers who held the rank of captain or below."

"So was Hans Bauer a captain?" asked Jamie when Dad had finished reading. "I don't know. All I know is that he won his medal on 25th December 1917."

"Wow. Christmas Day," said Jamie.

"Yes. Christmas Day exactly 99 years ago tomorrow," said Dad.

And despite, the roaring log fire that Mum had going in the lounge, I shivered.

Chapter 38

Naturally Jamie snaffled the medal declaring war was "men's stuff." Therefore the medal of an air ace couldn't be of any possible interest to girls. Corker and I begged to differ. Not because we really wanted Hans Baumer's Order of Merit, but simply to wind Jamie up and not allow him think he could just lay automatic claim to something we had all found.

Of course we quickly tired of our game, but not before we had won a couple of concessions. This year I would put out the slice of Christmas cake and beer for Santa. ("He's driving, surely it should be milk!" Corker protested.) And Corker would clean and chop the carrots for Rudolph, Donner, Blitzen, Prancer and Dancer and place her offering alongside mine on the hearth in the little lounge awaiting Santa's arrival down the chimney. Jamie agreed to the trade immediately, scoffing about "girls' stuff" as he dashed upstairs with his trophy to put it in pride of place on his bedroom windowsill.

There was absolutely no argument about the very last thing we did that night. Before climbing excitedly into our beds we each got one of Dad's long woollen socks – the grey ones he used for hill-walking – and tied them to our bedposts. Knowing that by morning they would be full of small, delicious surprises.

CHAPTER 39

Our surprise arrived long before morning and it was far from pleasant. At first I thought it was the house alarm and waited, pillow over head and fingers jammed in ears, for either Mum or Dad to get up and switch the infernal racket off.

When, after several minutes, it became clear that my parents were still in the land of nod, I unplugged my ears and listened more closely.

Though still dopey with tiredness, I gradually realised that the noise screeching through my brain was not the familiar electronic nee-naw of our house alarm. It was something entirely different. Something I had heard before when Mr Hogarth had played the class a video of the Blitz. It was the wail of an air-raid siren. But it was the pounding on the oak front door that finally stirred me into action. Of one thing I was certain as I jumped out of bed past the still empty sock, this wasn't Santa calling. The twins' joined me on the landing as the fog-horn voice boomed through the house. "I thought I told you younguns about lights. Lights must be extinguished during air raids, or I extinguish the folk that has them on." A short burst of piratical laughter followed and then the pounding restarted more violently than ever. We peeped over the balcony in growing horror as the door bulged and groaned under the force of the giant fist.

"We've got to get out of here," I yelled to the twins' above the banging.

"What about Mum and Dad. They'll help us," cried Corker.

"I can't really explain Corks, but this is only happening to us," I said.

"Even if they could hear or see it, I don't think there's anything they could do," I added, shepherding my brother and sister towards the stairs. For an eerie moment there was silence on the other side of the door.

Then the Warden's voice boomed out once more. "Final warning youn-guns. Open the door, or the shooting starts." Through the thick oak we could somehow hear every move the Warden was making. The sound of his great, calloused thumb unclipping the button on his holster. The weapon sliding out of the oiled leather. And the slow snicking back of the hammer as the sixgun was cocked ready for action.

"He's going to fire!" I screamed. "Run for your lives!" We charged down the stairs in a wild thrash of limbs launching ourselves into the back garden as the first gun shots crashed and echoed through the hall.

CHAPTER 40

Midnight on Christmas Eve in the Intensive Care Unit. A haven of peace and tranquillity. The corridor remained bathed in the same calming green glow. But a sprinkling of decorations had been added to lend a festive touch. Two large paper bells, one red and one yellow, hung from the ceiling. And the Ward Sister's small office now included a small artificial Christmas tree. Every few seconds the lights on it changed colour from silver to red to green to purple.

The Ward Sister had just returned from a carol service in the hospital chapel with tinsel on her uniform and a large smile on her cheerful face.

Her normally rosy cheeks had taken on an even deeper crimson tinge as she nodded in time to the nodding musical Santa singing "Jingle Bells" on her desk. Humming along with the tune, she sipped another kind of Bells from a tumbler usually hidden in the bandages cupboard. Her attention drifted to the plastic tree in the corner in front of a fresh supply of bedpans still in their polythene packaging.

Silver….red….green….purple. Silver….red….green….purple. The lights switched soothingly, restfully, hypnotically from one colour to the next amid the dark green plastic. Ah, peace and goodwill.

The Ward Sister gave an exhausted smile. After working five consecutive 12 hour shifts how she was looking forward to sliding beneath the crisp white sheets of her own bed, getting toasty-warm with the Electric Blanket on full blast, and slowly nodding off to a wonderfully long, undisturbed sleep well into her day off. Christmas Day off for the first time in four years. What unadulterated luxury! Silver….red….green…purple. Nodding. Nodding just like the nodding musical Santa, the Ward Sister's eyes started to close and her head – her impossibly heavy head – began to droop. "Jingle bells. Jingle bells. Jingle all the waaaaay."

But wait. Another bell was ringing and it wasn't Jingle Bells. It was the emergency bleeper. The Ward Sister's eyes sprang open and darted to the red light blinking and bleeping above her head. Tiredness forgotten. Festive merriness on hold. Fully alert and back on starched, efficient duty, she ran as fast as her squeaky rubber-soled shoes would carry her from her office into the patients' ward.

The green lines on the screen monitoring Robert Thomson's vital signs had become jagged mountains again. Only this time the peaks were even steeper, soaring from Ben Nevis to Mount Everest proportions. They were squashing up against each other and seemed to be coming almost too fast for the machine to cope with as Skankie, eyes wide with terror, chanted the same mantra "hands in the fire, hands in the fire."

CHAPTER 41

Corker clamped her hands over her ears and her lips formed to make words. But – although she was standing right next to me in the garden and clearly yelling at the top of her lungs - I couldn't hear a thing she was saying.

The reason was quite simple and at the same time utterly astonishing. The sky above our midnight garden had been transformed into an enormous fireworks display. Tracers of red dots streamed across the heavens followed by sudden gouts of orange and yellow flame in a constant barrage of deafening sound and colour.

The occasional thunderous KABOOM signalled a starburst of blinding white light, which turned night into day for a few dazzling seconds before the cloak of darkness descended once more. In a brief lull, Jamie's voice screamed in my ear, hoarse with excitement. "It's just like the old war films Alex."

"What is?" I shouted back.

"Bullets in the night," he said pointing up at the stream of red dots racing across the sky. " Ack-ack guns."

"Ack-ack. What's ack-ack?" I asked in bewilderment at what sounded like the silliest name in the world.

"Anti-aircraft guns," he said. But before I could consider the significance of his answer I heard the roar of a voice behind us somewhere in the house that I knew only too well.

"The Warden. He's coming for us." I mimed the last sentence as the night erupted into kaleidoscopic fury again. But the twins' needed no urging and we moved as fast as the snow would allow us down the garden.

Gradually we became aware of a new noise disguised beneath the crash and thunder of the anti-aircraft guns. At first it sounded a long way off and hesitant, like the geriatric cough and splutter of an old car backfiring. The backfiring ceased abruptly and was replaced by a low whine. The whine grew faster and closer, increasing to the shrill, teeth chattering screech of a machine teetering on the limits of breaking point.

I looked up into the night sky to see the plane miss the roof of our house by a matter of feet. All three of us automatically ducked, throwing ourselves to the ground and covering our heads as the undercarriage skimmed the treetops of our garden. Peeping between a fretwork of fingers I saw flames shooting from the stricken engines and for a fleeting second the fire illuminated the grey fuselage and the insignia of a black swastika before the plane disappeared beyond the trees.

We were up immediately and ploughing through the snow again. We cleared the holly bush in time to see the plane crash in a storm of fire and twisted metal.

"The school," shrieked Corker, "what's happened to the school?" It was true. The school at the bottom of our garden had vanished. In its place were rolling fields as far as the eye could see and in the centre of this foreign landscape lay the wreck of a burning German bomber with the flames licking along the wings towards the petrol tanks. Our attention had been so riveted on the plane that we had completely ignored everything else. But now, little by little, we were becoming aware of our immediate surroundings.

Our garden had also changed. The hurricane lamp Mum had put in the loft along with the wireless was now hanging at the entrance to the shelter. It shimmered blue in the darkness and behind its light inside the shelter I could make out huddled shapes. Human shapes.

Suddenly a man emerged. He stood for a moment beside the lamp and I caught the merest glimpse of a long face and a sharp nose beneath which sat a thick, bristling moustache.

The peaked bill of an army cap was snapped down over his eyes and he wore the uniform of an officer. Across his chest a row of medals glinted dully in the reflection of the blue light. He half turned at a sound only he seemed to hear and a small woman holding a baby joined him at the entrance. She grabbed his sleeve as if to pull him back inside the shelter and a desperate argument began.

Then the lanky boy I had glimpsed in the garden in what seemed years rather than only a couple of nights before came out of the shelter and also started pleading with the officer. "It's the family from the photograph. The old photograph in the loft!" I gasped. Jamie gave a mute nod and Corker stared so hard it appeared she was looking right through them. But her lips were moving and through the crash of guns and exploding shells I gradually made out the words she was repeating over and over again. "Hans in the fire. Hans in the fire."

Perhaps it was a trick of the light, but the officer seemed to halt for a second in the midst of his argument, turn and look directly at Corker. Then, with an almost imperceptible nod, he broke free of the woman's grasp and ran through the snow towards the burning plane.

After that everything seemed to happen all at once. Without any sign of hesitation the officer plunged through the flames and, casting his cap aside, began climbing along the wing to the cockpit. A fresh spout of flame erupted obscuring him from view for what seemed like an age.

Just when we started to think all hope was gone and that he must surely have perished, a figure re-appeared stumbling through the fire.

"His hair's on fire!" I screamed as the officer emerged from the inferno surrounded by a halo of flames.

"What's he got on his back," croaked Jamie.

"I think… I think it's the pilot," I said and at that moment the officer's legs appeared to buckle under his burden.

"No!" I yelled. "The petrol tank. The plane's going to explode. If he falls they'll die."

But as we watched in horrified fascination the officer, drawing on the last dregs of his strength, somehow managed to straighten his legs and hoist the injured pilot further up his back. Then with a final superhuman effort he forced himself forward in a crab-like scuttle away from the wreckage.

With a dull whump the petrol tanks exploded in a tower of orange flames and flying shrapnel.

The pair collapsed in a smouldering heap in the snow as the gutted skeleton of the plane continued to burn steadily behind them and a pall of acrid smoke curled into the night sky.

By the light of the glimmering funeral pyre we got our first sight of the pilot as the two bodies slowly untwined. He was still wearing his leather flying helmet, but his goggles were down around his neck to reveal piercing, hawk-like eyes that already looked alert, despite the terrible ordeal he had just endured. Climbing slowly to his feet, we could see that he was at least as tall as his rescuer.

He was dressed in dark overalls and a leather jacket with fur at the collar which was still smouldering. He swotted at the collar to stifle the flames and as he did so his jacket swung open for a second and I instantly recognised the small ribboned cross on his chest. "The Order of Merit," I whispered in awe. Then in a louder voice to the twins' I gasped. "The pilot. It's the air ace Dad told us about. It's Hans Baumer."

CHAPTER 42

Before I could make any further comment a chillingly familiar voice boomed in the night behind us. "Lights cost lives. Jerries bomb innocent women and children. But not tonight. I'll save you from the Hun." The three of us turned to see the hulking figure of the Warden crashing through the holly bush. Only there was something very different about him. He remained the giant we had first seen under the lamplight on our front lawn. But now his massive head lolled back and forth at an impossible angle as if he no longer had the power to lift it. And, instead of a whistle, a course rope was looped around his bull-like neck. Drawn so tight that it had cut into the thick folds of flesh. As his boots waded through the snow in great lolloping strides I noticed something else strange. He made no footprints. But the Warden had his sixgun out of the holster, the hammer was cocked, and he was waving it menacingly in the direction of the pilot.

Then I saw the army officer stagger to his feet. In the guttering light of the plane crash I could see his injuries were terrible. His uniform was charred beyond recognition, the knee length leather boots looked as if they had melted on his legs, and his sharp features had been transformed into a bloody Halloween mask. But he shambled forward in front of the pilot, his body shielding the German from the Warden's gun.

From the corner of one eye, I saw the long shadow caught in the blue hurricane lamp. Then the boy was in front of me, arms outsretched, running towards the army officer. After that I heard no sound. The bullet emerged from the barrel of the Warden's gun in silent slow motion. It seemed to hang in the air for an age before it finally found its target. The back of the boy's woollen balaclava helmet moved forward as if it had been ruffled by no more than a puff of wind. His white, skinny legs gave way almost gracefully as his body slumped into the snow in a tiny storm of powder crystals. When the dark stain on the woollen helmet spread to the snow the woman's mouth opened wide and she began to scream. Then the baby started bawling too. But no sound emerged and their grief was silent to our ears.

Like a giant marionette, whose strings have been spliced, the Warden slumped to his knees, his head flopping on his chest. All energy drained. Then painfully slowly, as if suddenly remembering a last task that still had to be accomplished, he forced himself to his feet and turned around. His eyes now bulged from their sockets like a cartoon character; the blood vessels having exploded and cracked into a series of criss-crossing dark rivers. His murderous gaze found us and with a final, soundless foghorn roar, he brought up his gun and fired.

I sensed rather than saw my little sister fall. One second she was standing beside me, the next there was an empty space and I looked down to see Corker's body lying slumped and lifeless in the snow. My anguished cry had sound. Jamie jumped as though he had been jabbed by a six inch needle.

"The Warden's shot Corker," I screamed. "We must help her Jamie."

But to my horror Jamie started to sprint away from us as fast as the drifts would allow. "Stop Jamie. Come back. Don't leave us," I yelled as I knelt beside Corker, while my brother's figure receded fast towards the bottom of the garden. He ran straight for the shed, threw open the door and disappeared inside. Why was he doing that? It made no sense. He would be trapped in there and after the Warden had polished me off, Jamie would be next. Then I heard the gruff roar of the engine and next minute Mum's Fire-engine red motorised lawn mower was crashing through the shed doors with Jamie in the driver's seat. The machine weaved drunkenly up the garden and seemed to go straight through the officer and pilot – although that must have been a trick of the light. It roared past the shelter going at least five miles an hour past the woman and baby standing like statues in the entrance. And circled the boy's body lying still in the snow before homing in on Corker and I.

But the Warden was beginning to move again, brandishing his gun, he closed in. I stood guard over my sister's body, determined to protect her to the end. The Warden raised the pistol, and aimed it directly at me. I could see his thick, calloused thumb pulling back the hammer and the chambers in the barrel revolving as the weight of his finger pressed down on the trigger.

The flower pot hit the Warden's gun hand at the precise second he fired the gun. The bullet went up in the air, ricocheting harmlessly into a tree bringing down a mini avalanche of snow and branches on the giant's head.

"Bullseye!" I cheered. "Way to go Jamie," as my brave little brother launched another pot. The Warden ducked and the missile missed, smashing harmlessly against the side of the shelter. But he lost his balance and fell full length in the snow giving Jamie precious seconds to control the mower.

"Quick!" he yelled jumping down from the driver's seat. "Help me get her in." Between us we somehow managed to heave the dead weight of the unconscious Corker aboard and jumped on on either side of her. Jamie released the brake and we roared off around the holly bush in a cloud of diesel fumes.

"Head for the house. It's our only chance," I shouted above the noise of the engine.

"L…look Alex!" cried Jamie pointing a shaking finger at Tumble Cottage as we cleared the fir trees. "It's disappearing!"

As we looked up the garden towards the house our bedrooms appeared to be fading in and out of reality. One minute the walls and tiled roof were there, the next the bricks and mortar where the twins' bedroom should have been was gone and we were staring at the empty black sky.

"The French windows…. the new kitchen…the lounge," it's all fading away Jamie."

The answer struck me like a thunderbolt. The ack-ack guns, the air raid, the plane crash. We had somehow gone back in time seventy five years to the Second World War. In 1940 Tumble Cottage was exactly that - a cottage. There was no new extension then.

"Faster Jamie!" I yelled. "We must get back inside now. Everything will be okay if we get inside."

The alarm in my voice must have been infectious because Jamie stamped his foot down even harder, threatening to push the accelerator pedal through the floor. The mower roared forward and up to its top speed of 12 miles and hour on its last lap up the garden.

A sixth sense made me turn around and there only a few yards behind us was the Warden. He looked literally on his last legs as he ploughed through the snow in great, ponderous steps. The rope was now pulled tight under his chin and the frayed end was upright behind his head as if an invisible hand was attempting to hoist him into the air. His face was a death white agony full of grinding teeth. But both his bloodless hands clutched the gun and as I watched he fired the sixth and last bullet. Again there was no sound. I saw it emerge from the barrel in exactly the same paralysingly slow journey the bullet aimed at the boy had made. I could see it spinning and turning in the air, the sharp brass point growing bigger and bigger as it propelled directly towards my head. Then six inches from my face, close enough to see the marks on the metal casing, the bullet simply stopped and dropped out of the air.

At precisely the same instant the Warden vanished into thin air. Jamie told me later that I screamed, which was the reason why he lost control of the mower, sending it crashing through the Christmas tree in a spray of tinsel and white lights.

My last memory was of lying on a cold slab – not in a mortuary - but on my back on the patio staring up at the sky. The starburst of shells had disappeared to be replaced by real stars. The heavens were full of them, but one appeared nearer and seemed to shine more brightly than the rest. Then I realised it wasn't a star at all, but the cross, Hans Baumer's medal, that glimmered with a brilliant radiance on the windowsill of Jamie's bedroom.

CHAPTER 43

I awoke to another miracle on that amazing Christmas Day – Corker bouncing around the bottom of my bed waving a wand and wearing a sparkling white fairy costume.

"Santa's been Alex…. The cake and the carrots are gone. He left my presents, see." And she did a twirl before collapsing on top of me in a swirl of sequins. "I see," I said hugging my sister so tight she squeaked in protest as the tears flowed down my cheeks. But I didn't see at all. I had been sure the Warden had killed my sister the night before in the garden when he fired his six gun and now here she was larger than life and bursting with excitement.

Then a large box crashed into my room followed by my equally delirious little brother. "Don't tell me, let me guess," I laughed. "The X Box."

"Right first time sis," he said, getting ready to make my bed a trampoline.

"Wait. Slow down," I said mouthing at Jamie, as Corker did a passable impression of the Sugar Plum Fairy and pirouetted from the room.

"Corker. She's okay. We thought she was dead. No bullet holes? How?"

"He never shot her. She fainted that was all," said Jamie brushing aside the subject as though our sister encountered murderous giants on a daily basis.

"Come on Alex. Come and open your presents. Mum and Dad are waiting in the lounge. And waiting in the lounge with Mum and Dad, after I had torn the wrapping paper away, was a gleaming yellow bicycle with purple mud guards. Supercool or what!

As Dad adjusted the saddle to my height, I glanced through the French Windows and saw the wreck of the Christmas tree lying in a tangle of broken fairy lights.

Dad caught the direction of my look. "It must have been windy last night. Heaven knows your Mum and I were out for the count.

A few smashed bulbs I'm afraid, but don't worry sweetheart, I'll replace them and we'll have the tree up again in no time."

The Christmas tree wasn't what I was worried about. I signalled to the twins' and we sneaked into the garden fearing the worst.

But there was nothing horrible to be seen. The Warden had vanished without trace. Equally, there was no sign of a burnt out German bomber sitting in the middle of rolling fields. We heaved a sigh of relief that the school was back in its normal place and in its usual vandalised condition.

Our greatest dread was finding the bodies of the burnt men. Worse.

The poor murdered boy still lying in the snow with the dark stain spreading behind his head. Only in daylight the stain wouldn't be anonymous black anymore, but blood red and we doubted whether we could stand such a terrible sight.

Thankfully, again there wasn't so much as a footprint or dent in the snow to show where they had been. It was the same for the woman and baby. And though we searched the shelter from top to bottom we found no trace of the hurricane lamp or wireless.

But returning to the house, Jamie spotted the mower at the side of the garage and we agreed to push it back to the shed before Mum and Dad discovered it had ever been moved. We paused at the overturned Christmas tree, staring wordlessly at the site of our near disaster. "Even with this mess, it's still hard to believe the things we saw. The things that happened," I said. The twins' nodded agreement. "Before I passed out I saw the medal on the windowsill. It was shining, glowing as if, as if it was on fire," I added, and we all looked up at the twins' bedroom window. The blackened cross glinted dully in the winter sun, but there was no hint of a supernatural glow. "We better get back inside before Mum and Dad wonder why we're not playing with our presents," I said.

"What's this?" asked Corker as she knelt in the snow beside the Christmas tree. At first I thought she had found another broken fairy light. But the object in her palm had a dull sheen – brass rather than silver.

"That's the Warden's last shot!" exclaimed Jamie. "The bullet he fired at you Alex. The one that fell out of the air." There was no doubt about it. The casing had exactly the same scratch marks I had seen the night before when the bullet was within inches of my face.

"You should keep it as a memento," laughed Jamie. "Give it to her Corker."

"No! Throw it away. Throw it as far as possible Corks. I never want to see it again," I screamed, rushing into the house.

Of course there was a final detail we all knew had to be checked. Later we crept up into the loft. The hurricane lamp was there and so was the wireless. They looked as dusty and broken down as the first time we laid eyes on them. Yet somehow they had been returned to the shelter in perfect working order. We no longer doubted what we had witnessed with our own eyes and ears during the past seven dramatic nights at Tumble Cottage. But we felt no nearer to solving the mystery of why we had experienced the events, or what they signified. Then we found the real reason for our visit to the loft. Scrunched together, heads touching in order to get a better look, we examined the old photograph under the spotlight of Mum's torch. The faces in the sepia-toned picture swam before our eyes as the images came alive and moved again before us. None of us were in any doubt. The tall proud army officer, the small, dark-haired woman holding the baby, the lanky boy with the balaclava helmet. They were undeniably the same people we had seen the night before at the bottom of our garden. The family that had lived in Tumble Cottage more than half a century ago had come back to haunt us. Why?

We could not imagine the answer to that question. So, like any other normal children, we decided to put these unfathomable events behind us and get on with having a great Christmas Day.

First though, we had to endure the torture of going to church. The routine was the same every year. Mum insisted we all had to dress up in our best clothes and attend the Christmas Day service in order to, in her words, "remember what Christmas was really about – giving rather than receiving." After we had "given" an hour listening to how Jesus was born and singing hymns, we were allowed to return to our presents. Lunch was a quick sandwich and then Dad suggested a family bicycle ride across nearby Epsom Downs to "blow away the cobwebs" before settling down to Christmas Dinner.

The twins' were luke-warm about the idea, but were bribed with the promise of a pit stop for ice cream at the half way point. I leapt at the chance to try out my brand new bicycle and muffled against the biting cold we cycled our favourite cross country route from the race course to the duck pond at Walton-on-the-Hill and back again.

Christmas afternoon assumed its cosily familiar routine. During the Queen's speech Dad lay snoring in the lounge following his third beer. Mum was busy in the kitchen cooking the turkey. We confined ourselves to the little lounge. Corker became the Sugar Plum Fairy again, practising spells and waving her wand enthusiastically at Jamie in the cheerful expectation of him turning into a frog. And Jamie graciously allowed me a five- minute shot on his X Box every half hour or so.

We were in the middle of an argument about how selfish my little brother was when the doorbell rang.

Chapter 44

"Four o'clock on Christmas afternoon. Who can this be?" tutted Mum as she swept through the hall wiping her hands on her apron. We crowded round behind her curious to see who this unexpected visitor might be on such a private family day. Mum opened the door to reveal a slight, elderly white-haired woman smiling benignly under the glow of the yellow lamp.

"Can I help you? Are you lost? We've just moved into the street. So I'm afraid we won't be much use if you're looking for a name," said Mum looking quizzically at the stranger.

"No I'm not lost," said the old woman kindly. I believe I have found the correct house and the right family. I'm looking for your children Mrs Madden. I wanted to thank them personally for all the kindness they showed my father," she added, looking past Mum to the three of us. "They were a great blessing to him at the end. He told me so. His name was Robert Thomson. I'm his daughter Rose."

As Mum bustled around the kitchen making tea for our guest, Skankie's daughter sat in our midst at the table. "First of all, I came to tell you that my father died last night. You were his friends and I knew you would want to know." She spoke so quietly that we strained to hear her voice above the rising hiss of the kettle.

"Secondly, I saw the same things that you saw," she said, fixing us with friendly eyes.

"How could that be?" I whispered matching her soft tones as the kettle gradually came to the boil.

"The baby you heard crying in the garden Alex? That was me. I was the baby in the old picture you found in the shelter."

"The shawl!" exclaimed Corker. "The letters RT. It wasn't Radio Times Jamie. They stood for your name, Rose Thomson!"

The old woman smiled and nodded her head. "You are the cleverest little girl Kristy – or can I call you Corker?

"How do you know my name? asked Corker.

"I know your brother and sister's names too - Jamie and Alex. I know everything about all of you," she said. "Like the amazing gifts you received from Santa. I love your fairy outfit Corker and Alex – your bicycle looks as if it could go faster than the wind. Unfortunately, I don't know very much about X boxes Jamie. I bet they are exciting too, but all these computer games are a bit too modern for me."

"What did you get for Christmas when you were a little girl?" asked Corker leaning closer to the old woman.

"Well my parents couldn't afford to buy my brother and I presents during the war. Toys in the shops were scarce and very expensive. But one Christmas, when I was about your age, my father made me a doll's house from an old birdcage with cardboard for the walls, and bits of a wastepaper basket for the roof. It even had a carpet made from a piece of hessian, that he had dyed red. And there were tables and chairs made from the pictures on cigarette cards. It was the most wonderful gift I had ever received," she said and her eyes grew moist. I never remember ever being happier than on that morning."

For a long moment Rose Thomson seemed to have returned to that special day as she softly sang the following words "There'll be blue birds over the white cliffs of Dover."

The shrill whistle of the kettle boiling made the three of us jump.

"Tea won't be a moment," called Mum from behind a gout of steam across the kitchen.

"Can I tempt you to a piece of Christmas cake?"

"No thank you Mrs Madden, tea will be perfect," said Rose Thomson inclining her head in Mum's direction. The movement was barely perceptible, but for a dizzying second I was staring at an empty chair. I shook my head not trusting my eyes and when I looked again the old woman was sitting exactly as she had before with her hands folded over the handbag in her lap. Too many late nights during the holidays, I thought.

The old woman was speaking again.

"The woman holding me in the photograph was my mother. The boy was my poor brother. And the old man you knew as Skankie was my father the army officer."

"I don't understand. How could that be?" I asked. "Skankie. Sorry Mr Thomson didn't live here. He lived along the road from us. And he didn't have any army title. He was plain mister." "He was originally a colonel," said the old woman. "He served at El Alamein with Monty."

The yellowing newspaper picture Mum and I found in the tea chest sprang unbidden into my mind followed by the image of the boastful Mrs Pelejic and her cats.

"The previous owner Mrs P told us about a colonel having lived here and his battle maps. Do you know where they are?" asked Jamie excitedly.

"That nasty Mrs Pelejic had them all the time dear," she said. "She took them with her along with the lights and the toilet fittings."

"How did you know…. Ouch," cried Jamie as I kicked him under the table.

The kitchen suddenly felt cold. I slid my hand down the radiator at my side, but it was piping hot, just like the night when the twins' door was frozen locked.

"Let me go on with my story and everything will become clear," said Rose Thomson. "My father had just returned home on leave to be with us and at that stage we indeed did live in this house, Tumble Cottage. It was his first night back when the air raid happened. He didn't even have time to change out of his uniform when the sirens went off.

"We all rushed down the garden to the shelter. We made it just in time. First, there was the terrible noise of the guns and then we heard the whine of the plane before we saw it. The next sound was the crash as it landed in the field. My mother and brother tried to stop father from going. But he wouldn't listen. Another human being needed help. To father it didn't matter that the man was a German, or that he was bombing our country.

The pilot was doing his duty just as my father had done his at El Alamein. So father saved Hans Baumer from the wreckage and suffered terrible injuries as you three children saw when you visited him in hospital."

"But what about the medal? How did he come to get Hans Baumer's medal?" I asked.

"Like my father, Hans Baumer was a man of honour," she said. "He won the Order of Merit in the First World War when he was only 18. Do any of you remember the medal's other name?"

"The Order of Generosity," said Corker just beating Jamie to the draw.

"That's correct," smiled Rose Thomson. "Hans Baumer was a gallant man and he recognised the same gallantry and generosity in my father. Even though they were enemies the two men were kindred spirits and my father went through fire to save Hans Baumer."

"Hans in the fire," whispered Corker.

"Yes dear, Hans in the fire," repeated the old woman. So Baumer gave my father his most treasured possession as a reminder – a keepsake of the most generous act one human being can make for another.

"My father never recovered physically or mentally from the fire. He spent years in hospitals and nursing homes. We couldn't afford to live in Tumble Cottage any longer and had to move. When Hans Baumer heard of my father's plight he visited him and then sent money to allow my father to live in a house at least near to the scene of so many memories. Even so it was too much for my mother and she died of a broken heart many years ago."

"And the Warden. Was he real?" I stammered.

The old woman's face grew paler at the mention of the giant of our waking nightmares.

"Oh yes dear. He was real all right. His name was John Crow and he was the most evil of men. He did many wicked things before he shot my poor brother in the garden. He was hanged for that terrible crime. Hanged by the neck until he was dead," she said and for the briefest blink she seemed to fade from the kitchen once more.

"You asked about my father being plain mister. After my brother was murdered he never wanted to be reminded of military things again. He took his battle maps down from the walls, burned his uniform and never answered to the title of colonel from that day forward."

The old woman unclasped her hands and got up from the chair.

"But you haven't touched your tea," protested Mum as Rose Thomson moved to the door. "Thank you Mrs Madden, but I have a long way to go. I only wanted to thank your children for their generosity. After all it's the time of year for peace and goodwill."

"Her shawl. The baby shawl. Surely she'd like it as a keepsake," said Corker tearing upstairs to her bedroom. Seconds later she was back in the hall and the three of us rushed outside.

Rose Thomson was at the bottom of the path under the street light. Somehow the lampost looked smaller and old fashioned as though it was made out of iron. She turned when we called, smiled and raised her hand to wave. But she kept on walking. We watched until she disappeared from view. Then Mum was calling us inside "before you catch your deaths." Before I closed our door I looked down the path at our beautiful garden. Like the Warden, Rose Thomson had made no footprints in the snow.

Chapter 45

Old Mangy, Rat's Tail, and Youngblood never did return to our garden. But their beautiful cubs did and we christened them Skankie, Hans and Rose in memory of the ghosts who had made such a powerful impression on our first Christmas at Tumble Cottage. Noodles came back too - though we saw him less often. When we did his coat had changed from grey to white, as white as the driven snow.

Later that spring there was a wild storm, the worst in years. The windows shook, the old rafters creaked, and the house groaned like a ship at sea. But we all slept soundly. For we all knew that the noises were nothing more than nature steering the house safely through the night. The spirits surrounding Tumble Cottage had vanished and were finally resting in peace.

But if we needed a sign we got it the following morning when Mum called us from the bottom of the garden. She looked slightly sad as she stood in her gardening gloves, hands on hips, surveying the wreckage of the air raid shelter. The corrugated roof had been torn open like a sardine tin and the walls had collapsed inwards on to the old concrete floor.

"Well it did what it was built to do, I suppose," she sighed. It doesn't owe anyone anything. But now I'll have to find somewhere else to store my logs."

56317215R00102

Made in the USA
Charleston, SC
17 May 2016